ROSS MACDONALD

The Moving Target

Ross Macdonald's real name was Kenneth Millar. Born near San Francisco in 1915 and raised in Vancouver, British Columbia, Millar returned to the U.S. as a young man and published his first novel in 1944. He served as the president of the Mystery Writers of America and was awarded their Grand Master Award, as well as the Mystery Writers of Great Britain's Silver Dagger Award. He died in 1983.

The Moving Target

ROSS MACDONALD

The Moving Target

Vintage Crime/Black Lizard

Vintage Books

A Division of Random House, Inc.

New York

FIRST VINTAGE CRIME/BLACK LIZARD EDITION,
MARCH 1998

Copyright © 1949, copyright renewed 1977 by Ross Macdonald

Library of Congress Cataloging-in-Publication Data
Macdonald, Ross, 1915–
The moving target / by Ross Macdonald.
p.   cm.—(Vintage crime/Black Lizard)
ISBN 978-0-375-70146-7
1. Archer, Lew (Fictitious character)—Fiction. 2. Private
investigators—California—Fiction. I. Title. II. Series.
PS3525.I486M67   1998
813'.52—dc21   97-47422
CIP

Random House Web address: www.randomhouse.com

Printed in the United States of America

The Moving Target

chapter **1**   The cab turned off U.S. 101 in the direction of the sea. The road looped round the base of a brown hill into a canyon lined with scrub oak.

"This is Cabrillo Canyon," the driver said.

There weren't any houses in sight. "The people live in caves?"

"Not on your life. The estates are down by the ocean."

A minute later I started to smell the sea. We rounded another curve and entered its zone of coolness. A sign beside the road said: "Private Property: Permission to pass over revocable at any time."

The scrub oak gave place to ordered palms and Monterey cypress hedges. I caught glimpses of lawns effervescent with sprinklers, deep white porches, roofs of red tile and green copper. A Rolls with a doll at the wheel went by us like a gust of wind, and I felt unreal.

The light-blue haze in the lower canyon was like a thin smoke from slowly burning money. Even the sea looked precious through it, a solid wedge held in the canyon's mouth, bright blue and polished like a stone. Private property: color guaranteed fast; will not shrink egos. I had never seen the Pacific look so small.

We turned up a drive between sentinel yews, cruised round in a private highway network for a while, and came out above the sea stretching deep and wide to Hawaii. The house stood part way down the shoulder of the bluff, with its back to the canyon. It was long and low. Its wings met at an obtuse angle pointed at the sea like a massive white arrowhead. Through screens of shrubbery I caught the white glare of tennis courts, the blue-green shimmer of a pool.

The driver turned on the fan-shaped drive and stopped beside the garages. "This is where the cavemen live. You want the service entrance?"

"I'm not proud."

"You want me to wait?"

"I guess so."

A heavy woman in a blue linen smock came out on the service porch and watched me climb out of the cab. "Mr. Archer?"

"Yes. Mrs. Sampson?"

"Mrs. Kromberg: I'm the housekeeper." A smile passed over her lined face like sunlight on a plowed field. "You can let your taxi go. Felix can drive you back to town when you're ready."

I paid off the driver and got my bag out of the back. I felt a little embarrassed with it in my hand. I didn't know whether the job would last an hour or a month.

"I'll put your bag in the storeroom," the housekeeper said. "I don't think you'll be needing it."

She led me through a chromium-and-porcelain kitchen, down a hall that was cool and vaulted like a cloister, into a cubicle that rose to the second floor when she pressed a button.

"All the modern conveniences," I said to her back.

"They had to put it in when Mrs. Sampson hurt her legs. It cost seven thousand, five hundred dollars."

If that was supposed to silence me, it did. She knocked on a door across the hall from the elevator. Nobody answered. After knocking again, she opened the door on a high white room too big and bare to be feminine. Above the massive bed there was a painting of a clock, a map, and a woman's hat arranged on a dressing-table. Time, space, and sex. It looked like a Kuniyoshi.

The bed was rumpled but empty. "Mrs. Sampson!" the housekeeper called.

A cool voice answered her: "I'm on the sun deck. What do you want?"

"Mr. Archer's here—the man you sent the wire to."

"Tell him to come out. And bring me some more coffee."

"You go out through the French windows," the housekeeper said, and went away.

Mrs. Sampson looked up from her book when I stepped out. She was half lying on a chaise longue with her back to the late morning sun, a towel draped over her body. There was a wheelchair standing beside her, but she didn't look like an invalid. She was very lean and brown, tanned so dark that her flesh seemed hard. Her hair was bleached, curled tightly on her narrow head like blobs of whipped cream. Her age was as hard to tell as the age of a figure carved from mahogany.

She dropped the book on her stomach and offered me her

hand. "I've heard about you. When Millicent Drew broke with Clyde, she said you were helpful. She didn't exactly say how."

"It's a long story," I said. "And a sordid one."

"Millicent and Clyde are dreadfully sordid, don't you think? These æsthetic men! I've always suspected his mistress wasn't a woman."

"I never think about my clients." With that I offered her my boyish grin, a little the worse for wear.

"Or talk about them?"

"Or talk about them. Even with my clients."

Her voice was clear and fresh, but the sickness was there in her laugh, a little clatter of bitterness under the trill. I looked down into her eyes, the eyes of something frightened and sick hiding in the fine brown body. She lowered the lids.

"Sit down, Mr. Archer. You must be wondering why I sent for you. Or don't you wonder either?"

I sat on a deck chair beside the chaise. "I wonder. I even conjecture. Most of my work is divorce. I'm a jackal, you see."

"You slander yourself, Mr. Archer. And you don't talk like a detective, do you? I'm glad you mentioned divorce. I want to make it clear at the start that divorce is not what I want. I want my marriage to last. You see, I intend to outlive my husband."

I said nothing, waiting for more. When I looked more closely, her brown skin was slightly roughened, slightly withered. The sun was hammering her copper legs, hammering down on my head. Her toenails and her fingernails were painted the same blood color.

"It mayn't be survival of the fittest. You probably know I can't use my legs any more. But I'm twenty years younger than he is, and I'm going to survive him." The bitterness had come through into her voice, buzzing like a wasp.

She heard it and swallowed it at a gulp. "It's like a furnace out here, isn't it? It's not fair that men should have to wear coats. Please take yours off."

"No, thanks."

"You're very gentlemanly."

"I'm wearing a shoulder holster. And still wondering. You mentioned Albert Graves in your telegram."

"He recommended you. He's one of Ralph's lawyers. You can talk to him after lunch about your pay."

"He isn't D.A. any more?"

"Not since the war."

"I did some work for him in '40 and '41. I haven't seen him since."

"He told me. He told me you were good at finding people." She smiled a white smile, carnivorous and startling in her dark face. "Are you good at finding people, Mr. Archer?"

" 'Missing persons' is better. Your husband's missing?"

"Not missing, exactly. Just gone off by himself, or in company. He'd be frantically angry if I went to the Missing Persons Bureau."

"I see. You want me to find him if possible and identify the company. And what then?"

"Just tell me where he is, and with whom. I'll do the rest myself." Sick as I am, said the little whining undertone, legless though I be.

"When did he go away?"

"Yesterday afternoon."

"Where?"

"Los Angeles. He was in Las Vegas—we have a desert place near there—but he flew to Los Angeles yesterday afternoon with Alan. Alan's his pilot. Ralph gave him the slip at the airport and went off by himself."

"Why?"

"I suppose because he was drunk." Her red mouth curved contemptuously. "Alan said he'd been drinking."

"You think he's gone off on a binge. Does he often?"

"Not often, but totally. He loses his inhibitions when he drinks."

"About sex?"

"All men do, don't they? But that isn't what concerns me. He loses his inhibitions about money. He tied one on a few months ago and gave away a mountain."

"A mountain?"

"Complete with hunting-lodge."

"Did he give it to a woman?"

"I almost wish he had. He gave it to a man, but it's not what you're thinking. A Los Angeles holy man with a long gray beard."

"He sounds like a soft touch."

"Ralph? He'd go stark staring mad if you called him that to his face. He started out as a wildcat oil operator. You know the type, half man, half alligator, half bear trap, with a piggy bank where his heart should be. That's when he's sober. But alcohol softens him up, at least it has the last few years. A few drinks, and he wants to be a little boy again. He goes looking for a mother type or a father type to blow his nose and dry away his tears and spank him when he's naughty. Do I sound cruel? I'm simply being objective."

"Yes," I said. "You want me to find him before he gives away another mountain." Dead or alive, I thought; but I wasn't her analyst.

"And if he's with a woman, naturally I'll be interested. I'll want to know all about her, because I couldn't afford to give away an advantage like that."

I wondered who her analyst was.

"Have you any particular woman in mind?"

"Ralph doesn't confide in me—he's much closer to Miranda than he is to me—and I'm not equipped to spy on him. That's why I'm hiring you."

"To put it bluntly," I said.

"I always put things bluntly."

chapter **2**   A Filipino houseboy in a white jacket appeared at the open French window. "Your coffee, Mrs. Sampson."

He set down the silver coffee service on a low table by the chaise. He was little and quick. The hair on his small round head was slick and black like a coating of grease.

"Thank you, Felix." She was gracious to her servants or making an impression on me. "Will you have some, Mr. Archer?"

"No, thanks."

"Perhaps you'd like a drink."

"Not before lunch. I'm the new-type detective."

She smiled and sipped her coffee. I got up and walked to the seaward end of the sun deck. Below it the terraces de-

scended in long green steps to the edge of the bluff, which
fell sharply down to the shore.

I heard a splash around the corner of the house and leaned
out over the railing. The pool was on the upper terrace, an
oval of green water set in blue tile. A girl and a boy were
playing tag, cutting the water like seals. The girl was chasing
the boy. He let her catch him.

Then they were a man and a woman, and the moving scene
froze in the sun. Only the water moved, and the girl's hands.
She was standing behind him with her arms around his waist.
Her fingers moved over his ribs gently as a harpist's, clenched
in the tuft of hair in the center of his chest. Her face was
hidden against his back. His face held pride and anger like a
blind bronze.

He pushed her hands down and stepped away. Her face
was naked then and terribly vulnerable. Her arms hung down
as if they had lost their purpose. She sat down on the edge of
the pool and dangled her feet in the water.

The dark young man did a flip and a half from the spring-
board. She didn't look. The drops fell off the tips of her hair
like tears and ran down into her bosom.

Mrs. Sampson called me by name. "You haven't had
lunch?"

"No."

"Lunch for three in the patio, then, Felix. I'll eat up here
as usual."

Felix bowed slightly and started away. She called him back.
"Bring the photo of Mr. Sampson from my dressing-room.
You'll have to know what he looks like, won't you, Mr.
Archer?"

The face in the leather folder was fat, with thin gray hair

and a troubled mouth. The thick nose tried to be bold and succeeded in being obstinate. The smile that folded the puffed eyelids and creased the sagging cheeks was fixed and forced. I'd seen such smiles in mortuaries on the false face of death. It reminded me that I was going to grow old and die.

"A poor thing, but mine own," said Mrs. Sampson.

Felix let out a little sound that could have been a snicker, grunt, or sigh. I couldn't think of anything to add to his comment.

He served lunch in the patio, a red-tiled triangle between the house and the hillside. Above the masonry retaining wall the slope was planted with ground cover, ageratum, and trailing lobelia in an unbreaking blue-green wave.

The dark young man was there when Felix led me out. He had laid away his anger and his pride, changed to a fresh light suit, and looked at ease. He was tall enough when he stood up to make me feel slightly undersized—six foot three or four. His grip was hard.

"Alan Taggert's my name. I pilot Sampson's plane."

"Lew Archer."

He rotated a small drink in his left hand. "What are you drinking?"

"Milk."

"No kidding? I thought you were a detective."

"Fermented mare's milk, that is."

He had a pleasant white smile. "Mine's gin and bitters. I picked up the habit at Port Moresby."

"Done a good deal of flying?"

"Fifty-five missions. And a couple of thousand hours."

"Where?"

"Mostly in the Carolines. I had a P-38."

He said it with loving nostalgia, like a girl's name.

The girl came out then, wearing a black-striped dress, narrow in the right places, full in the others. Her dark-red hair, brushed and dried, bubbled around her head. Her wide green eyes were dazzling and strange in her brown face, like light eyes in an Indian.

Taggert introduced her. She was Sampson's daughter Miranda. She seated us at a metal table under a canvas umbrella that grew out of the table's center on an iron stem. I watched her over my salmon mayonnaise; a tall girl whose movements had a certain awkward charm, the kind who developed slowly and was worth waiting for. Puberty around fifteen, first marriage or affair at twenty or twenty-one. A few hard years outgrowing romance and changing from girl to woman; then the complete fine woman at twenty-eight or thirty. She was about twenty-one, a little too old to be Mrs. Sampson's daughter.

"My stepmother—" she said, as if I'd been thinking aloud —"my stepmother is always going to extremes."

"Do you mean me, Miss Sampson? I'm a very moderate type."

"Not you, especially. Everything she does is extreme. Other people fall off horses without being paralyzed from the waist down. But not Elaine. I think it's psychological. She isn't the raving beauty she used to be, so she retired from competition. Falling off the horse gave her a chance to do it. For all I know, she deliberately fell off."

Taggert laughed shortly. "Come off it, Miranda. You've been reading a book."

She looked at him haughtily. "You'll never be accused of that."

"Is there a psychological explanation for my being here?"
I said.

"I'm not exactly sure why you're here. Is it to track Ralph
down, or something like that?"

"Something like that."

"I suppose she wants to get something on him. You have
to admit it's pretty extreme to call in a detective because a
man stays away overnight."

"I'm discreet, if that's what's worrying you."

"Nothing's worrying me," she said sweetly. "I merely made
a psychological observation."

The Filipino servant moved unobtrusively across the
patio. Felix's steady smile was a mask behind which his
personality waited in isolation, peeping furtively from the
depths of his bruised-looking black eyes. I had the feeling
that his pointed ears heard everything I said, counted my
breathing, and could pick up the beat of my heart on a clear
day.

Taggert had been looking uncomfortable, and changed the
subject abruptly. "I don't think I ever met a real-life detective
before."

"I'd give you my autograph, only I sign it with an 'X.'"

"Seriously, though, I'm interested in detectives. I thought
I'd like to be one at one time—before I went up in a plane.
I guess most kids dream about it."

"Most kids don't get stuck with the dream."

"Why? Don't you like your work?"

"It keeps me out of mischief. Let's see, you were with Mr.
Sampson when he dropped out of sight?"

"Right."

"How was he dressed?"

"Sports clothes. Harris tweed jacket, brown wool shirt, tan slacks, brogues. No hat."

"And when was this exactly?"

"About three thirty—when we landed at Burbank yesterday afternoon. They had to move another crate before I could park the plane. I always put it away myself; it's got some special gadgets we wouldn't want stolen. Mr. Sampson went to call the hotel to send out a limousine."

"What hotel?"

"The Valerio."

"The pueblo off Wilshire?"

"Ralph keeps a bungalow there," Miranda said. "He likes it because it's quiet."

"When I got out to the main entrance," Taggert continued, "Mr. Sampson was gone. I didn't think much about it. He'd been drinking pretty hard, but that was nothing unusual, and he could still look after himself. It made me a little sore, though. There I was stranded in Burbank, simply because he couldn't wait five minutes. It's a three-dollar taxi ride to the Valerio, and I couldn't afford that."

He glanced at Miranda to see if he was saying too much. She looked amused.

"Anyway," he said, "I took a bus to the hotel. Three buses, about half an hour on each. And then he wasn't there. I waited around until nearly dark, and then I flew the plane home."

"Did he ever get to the Valerio?"

"No. He hadn't been there at all."

"What about his luggage?"

"He didn't carry luggage."

"Then he wasn't planning to stay overnight?"

"It doesn't follow," Miranda put in. "He kept whatever he needed in the bungalow at the Valerio."

"Maybe he's there now."

"No. Elaine's been phoning every hour on the hour."

I turned to Taggert. "Didn't he say anything about his plans?"

"He was going to spend the night at the Valerio."

"How long was he by himself when you were parking the plane?"

"Fifteen minutes or so. Not more than twenty."

"The limousine from the Valerio would've had to get there pretty fast. He may never have called the hotel at all."

"Somebody might have met him at the airport," Miranda said.

"Did he have many friends in Los Angeles?"

"Business acquaintances mostly. Ralph's never been much of a mixer."

"Can you give me their names?"

She moved her hand in front of her face as if the names were insects. "You'd better ask Albert Graves. I'll call his office and tell him you're coming. Felix will drive you in. And then I suppose you'll be going back to Los Angeles."

"It looks like the logical place to start."

"Alan can fly you." She stood up and looked down at him with a flash of half-learned imperiousness. "You're not doing anything special this afternoon, are you, Alan?"

"Glad to," he said. "It'll keep me from getting bored."

She switch-tailed into the house, a pretty piece in a rage.

"Give her a break," I said.

He stood up and overshadowed me. "What do you mean?"

He had a trace of smugness, of high-school arrogance, and

I needled it. "She needs a tall man. You'd make a handsome pair."

"Sure, sure." He wagged his head negatively from side to side. "More people jump to conclusions about me and Miranda."

"Including Miranda?"

"I happen to be interested in somebody else. Not that it's any of your business. Or that God damn eight ball's either."

He meant Felix, who was standing in the doorway that led to the kitchen. He suddenly disappeared.

"The bastard gets on my nerves," Taggert said. "He's always hanging around and listening in."

"Maybe he's just interested."

He snorted. "He's just one of the things that gripes me about this place. I eat with the family, yeah, but don't think I'm not a servant when the chips are down. A bloody flying chauffeur."

Not to Miranda, I thought but didn't say it. "It's an easy enough job, isn't it? Sampson can't be flying much of the time."

"The flying doesn't bother me. I like it. What I don't like is being the old guy's keeper."

"He needs a keeper?"

"He can be hell on wheels. I couldn't tell you about him in front of Miranda, but the last week in the desert you'd think he was trying to drink himself to death. A quart and a pint a day. When he drinks like that he gets delusions of grandeur, and I get sick of taking chicken from a lush. Then he goes sentimental. He wants to adopt me and buy an airline for me." His voice went harsh and loose, in satiric mimicry of a drunk old man's: " 'I'll look after you, Alan boy. You'll get your airline.' "

"Or a mountain?"

"I'm not kidding about the airline. He could do it, too. But he doesn't give anything away when he's sober. Not a thin dime."

"Strictly schizo," I said. "What makes him like that?"

"I wouldn't know for sure. The bitch upstairs would drive anybody crazy. Then he lost a son in the war. That's where I come in, I guess. He doesn't really need a full-time pilot. Bob Sampson was a flier, too. Shot down over Sakashima. Miranda thinks that that's what broke the old man up."

"How does Miranda get along with him?"

"Pretty well, but they've been feuding lately. Sampson's been trying to make her get married."

"To anybody in particular?"

"Albert Graves." He said it deadpan, neither pro nor con.

chapter **3**   The highway entered Santa Teresa at the bottom of the town near the sea. We drove through a mile of slums: collapsing shacks and store-front tabernacles, dirt paths where sidewalks should have been, black and brown children playing in the dust. Nearer the main street there were a few tourist hotels with neon signs like icing on a cardboard cake, red-painted chili houses, a series of shabby taverns where the rumdums were congregating. Half the men in the street had short Indian bodies and morocco faces. After

Cabrillo Canyon I felt like a man from another planet. The Cadillac was a space ship skimming just above the ground.

Felix turned left at the main street, away from the sea. The street changed as we went higher. Men in colored shirts and seersucker suits, women in slacks and midriff dresses displaying various grades of abdomen, moved in and out of California Spanish shops and office buildings. Nobody looked at the mountains standing above the town, but the mountains were there, making them all look silly.

Taggert had been sitting in silence, his handsome face a blank. "How do you like it?" he asked me.

"I don't have to like it. How about you?"

"It's pretty dead for my money. People come here to die like elephants. But then they go on living—call it living."

"You should have seen it before the war. It's a hive of activity compared with what it was. There was nothing but rich old ladies clipping coupons and pinching pennies and cutting the assistant gardener's wages."

"I didn't know you knew the town."

"I worked on a couple of cases with Bert Graves—when he was District Attorney."

Felix parked in front of a yellow stucco archway that led into the courtyard of an office building. He opened the glass partition. "Mr. Graves's office is on the second floor. You can take the elevator."

"I'll wait out here," Taggert said.

Graves's office was a contrast to the grimy cubicle in the courthouse where he used to prepare his cases. The waiting-room was finished in cool green cloth and bleached wood. A blonde receptionist with cool green eyes completed the color scheme and said:

"Do you have an appointment, sir?"

"Just tell Mr. Graves it's Lew Archer."

"Mr. Graves is busy at the moment."

"I'll wait."

I sat down in an overstuffed chair and thought about Sampson. The blonde's white fingers danced on her typewriter keys. I was restless and still feeling unreal, hired to look for a man I couldn't quite imagine. An oil tycoon who consorted with holy men and was drinking himself to death. I pulled his photograph out of my pocket and looked at it again. It looked back at me.

The inner door was opened, and an old lady backed out bobbing and chortling. Her hat was something she'd found washed up on the beach. There were diamonds in the watch that was pinned to her purple silk bosom.

Graves followed her out. She was telling him how clever he was, very clever and helpful. He was pretending to listen. I stood up. When he saw me he winked at me over the hat.

The hat went away, and he came back from the door. "It's good to see you, Lew."

He didn't slap backs, but his grip was as hard as ever. The years had changed him, though. His hairline was creeping back at the temples, his small gray eyes peered out from a network of little wrinkles. The heavy blue-shadowed jaw was drooping at the sides in the beginning of jowls. It was unpleasant to remember that he wasn't five years older than I was. But Graves had come up the hard way, and that was an aging process.

I told him I was glad to see him. I was.

"It must be six or seven years," he said.

"All of that. You're not prosecuting any more."

"I couldn't afford to."

"Married?"

"Not yet. Inflation." He grinned. "How's Sue?"

"Ask her lawyer. She didn't like the company I kept."

"I'm sorry to hear it, Lew."

"Don't be." I changed the subject. "Doing much trial work?"

"Not since the war. It doesn't pay off in a town like this."

"Something must." I looked around the room. The cool blond girl permitted herself to smile.

"This is just my front. I'm still a struggling attorney. But I'm learning to talk to the old ladies." His smile was wry. "Come inside, Lew."

The inner office was bigger, cooler, more heavily furnished. There were hunting prints on the two bare walls. The others were lined with books. He looked smaller behind his massive desk.

"What about politics?" I said. "You were going to be Governor, remember?"

"The party's gone to pieces in California. Anyway, I've had my fill of politics. I ran a town in Bavaria for two years. Military Government."

"Carpetbagger, eh? I was Intelligence. Now what about Ralph Sampson?"

"You talked to Mrs. Sampson?"

"I did. It was quite an experience. But I don't quite get the point of this job. Do you?"

"I should. I talked her into it."

"Why?"

"Because Sampson might need protection. A man with five million dollars shouldn't take the chances he does. He's an alcoholic, Lew. He's been getting worse since his boy was killed, and sometimes I'm afraid he's losing his mind. Did she tell you about Claude, the character he gave the hunting-lodge to?"

"Yeah. The holy man."

"Claude seems to be harmless, but the next one might not be. I don't have to tell you about Los Angeles. It isn't safe for an elderly lush by himself."

"No," I said. "You don't have to tell me. But Mrs. Sampson seemed to think he's off on a round of pleasures."

"I encouraged her to think that. She wouldn't spend money to protect him."

"But you would."

"Her money. I'm just his lawyer. Of course, I rather like the old guy."

And hope to be his son-in-law, I thought.

"How much is she good for?"

"Whatever you say. Fifty a day and expenses?"

"Make it seventy-five. I don't like the imponderables in this case."

"Sixty-five." He laughed. "I've got to protect my client."

"I won't argue. There may not even be a case. Sampson could be with friends."

"I've tried them. He didn't have many friends here. I'll give you a list of contacts, but I wouldn't waste time on it except as a last resort. His real friends are in Texas. That's where he made his money."

"You're taking this pretty seriously," I said. "Why don't you go one step further and take it to the police?"

"Trying to talk yourself out of a job?"

"Yes."

"It can't be done, Lew. If the police found him for me, he'd fire me in a minute. And I can't be sure he isn't with a woman. Last year I found him in a fifty-dollar house in San Francisco."

"What were you doing there?"

"Looking for him."

"This smells more and more like divorce," I said. "But Mrs. Sampson insisted that isn't it. I still don't get it—or her."

"You can't expect to. I've known her for years and I don't understand her. But I can handle her, up to a point. If anything ticklish comes up, bring it to me. She has a few dominant motives, like greed and vanity. You can count on them when you're dealing with her. And she doesn't want a divorce. She'd rather wait and inherit all his money—or half of it. Miranda gets the other half."

"Were those always her dominant motives?"

"Ever since I've known her, since she married Sampson. She tried to have a career before that: dancing, painting, dress-designing. No talent. She was Sampson's mistress for a while, and finally she fell back on him, married him as a last resort. That was six years ago."

"And what happened to her legs?"

"She fell off a horse she was trying to train, and hit her head on a stone. She hasn't walked since."

"Miranda thinks she doesn't want to walk."

"Were you talking to Miranda?" His face lit up. "Isn't she a marvelous kid?"

"She certainly is." I stood up. "Congratulations."

He blushed and said nothing. I had never seen Graves blush before. I felt slightly embarrassed.

On the way down in the automatic elevator he asked me: "Did she say anything about me?"

"Not a word. I plucked it out of the air."

"She's a marvelous kid," he repeated. At forty he was drunk on love.

He sobered up in a hurry when we reached the car. Miranda was in the back seat with Alan Taggert. "I followed you in. I decided to fly down to Los Angeles with you. Hello, Bert."

"Hello, Miranda."

He gave her a hurt look. She was looking at Taggert. Taggert was looking nowhere in particular. It was a triangle, but not an equilateral one.

chapter **4**   We rose into the offshore wind sweeping across the airport and climbed toward the southern break in the mountains. Santa Teresa was a colored air map on the mountains' knees, the sailboats in the harbor white soap chips in a tub of bluing. The air was very clear. The peaks stood up so sharply that they looked like papier-mâché I could poke my finger through. Then we rose past them into chillier air and saw the wilderness of mountains stretching to the fifty-mile horizon.

The plane leaned gradually and turned out over the sea. It was a four-seater equipped for night flying. I was in the back seat. Miranda was in front on Taggert's right. She watched his right hand, careful on the stick. He seemed to take pride in holding the plane quiet and steady.

We hit a downdraft and fell a hundred feet. Her left hand grasped his knee. He let it stay there.

What was obvious to me must have been obvious to Albert Graves. Miranda was Taggert's if he wanted her, brain and body. Graves was wasting his time, building himself up to a very nasty letdown.

I knew enough about him to understand it. Miranda was everything he'd dreamed about—money, youth, bud-sharp breasts, beauty on the way. He'd set his mind on her and had to have her. All his life he'd been setting his mind on things —and getting them.

He was a farmer's son from Ohio. When he was fourteen or fifteen his father lost his farm and died soon after. Bert supported his mother by building tires in a rubber factory for six years. When she died he put himself through college and came out with a Phi Beta Kappa. Before he was thirty he had taken his law degree at the University of Michigan. He spent one year in corporation law in Detroit and decided to come west. He settled in Santa Teresa because he had never seen mountains or swum in the sea. His father had always intended to retire in California, and Bert inherited the Midwestern dream—which included the daughter of a Texas oil millionaire.

The dream was intact. He'd worked too hard to have any time for women. Deputy D. A., City Attorney, D. A. He prepared his cases as if he was laying the foundations of society. I knew, because I'd helped him. His courtroom work had been cited by a state-supreme-court judge as a model of forensic jurisprudence. And now at forty Graves had decided to beat his head against a wall.

But perhaps he could scale the wall, or the wall would fall

down by itself. Taggert shook his leg like a horse frightening flies. The plane veered and returned to its course. Miranda removed her hand.

With a little angry flush spreading to his ears, Taggert pulled the stick and climbed—climbed as if he could leave her behind and be all alone in the heart of the sky. The thermometer in the roof sank below forty. At eight thousand feet I could see Catalina far down ahead to the right. After a few minutes we turned left toward the white smudge of Los Angeles.

I shouted over the roar: "Can you set her down at Burbank? I want to ask some questions."

"I'm going to."

The summer heat of the valley came up to meet us as we circled in. Heat lay like a fine ash on the rubbish lots and fields and half-built suburbs, slowing the tiny cars on the roads and boulevards, clogging the air. The impalpable white dust invaded my nostrils and dried my throat. Dryness of the throat went with the feeling I always had, even after half a day, when I came back to the city.

The taxi starter at the airport wore steel-wire armbands on the sleeves of his red-striped shirt. A yellow cap hung almost vertically from the back of his gray head. Seasons of sun and personal abuse had given him an angry red face and an air of great calm.

He remembered Sampson when I showed him the photograph.

"Yeah, he was here yesterday. I noticed him because he was a little under the weather. Not blotto, or I would of called a guard. Just a couple of drinks too many."

"Sure," I said. "Was anybody with him?"

"Not that I saw."

A woman wearing two foxes that looked as if they had died from the heat broke out of the line at the curb. "I have to get downtown right away."

"Sorry, madam. You got to wait your turn."

"I tell you this is urgent."

"You got to wait your turn," he said monotonously. "We got a cab shortage, see?"

He turned to me again. "Anything else, bud? This guy in trouble or something?"

"I wouldn't know. How did he leave?"

"By car—a black limousine. I noticed it because it didn't carry no sign. Maybe from one of the hotels."

"Was there anybody in it?"

"Just the driver."

"You know him?"

"Naw. I know some of the hotel drivers, but they're always changing. This was a little guy, I think, kind of pale."

"You don't remember the make or the license number?"

"I keep my eyes open, bud, but I ain't a genius."

"Thanks." I gave him a dollar. "Neither am I."

I went upstairs to the cocktail bar, where Miranda and Taggert were sitting like strangers thrown together by accident.

"I called the Valerio," Taggert said. "The limousine should be here any minute."

The limousine, when it came, was driven by a pale little man in a shiny blue-serge suit like an umpire's and a cloth cap. The taxi starter said he wasn't the man who had picked up Sampson the day before.

I got into the front seat with him. He turned with nervous quickness, gray-faced, concave-chested, convex-eyed. "Yes, sir?" The question trailed off gently and obsequiously.

"We're going to the Valerio. Were you on duty yesterday afternoon?"

"Yes, sir." He shifted gears.

"Was anybody else?"

"No, sir. There's another fellow on the night shift, but he doesn't come on till six."

"Did you have any calls to the Burbank airport yesterday afternoon?"

"No, sir." A worried expression was creeping into his eyes and seemed to suit them. "I don't believe I did."

"But you're not certain."

"Yes, sir. I'm certain. I didn't come out this way."

"You know Ralph Sampson?"

"At the Valerio? Yes, sir. Indeed I do, sir."

"Have you seen him lately?"

"No, sir. Not for several weeks."

"I see. Tell me, who takes the calls for you?"

"The switchboard operator. I do hope there's nothing wrong, sir. Is Mr. Sampson a friend of yours?"

"No," I said. "I'm one of his employees."

All the rest of the way he drove in tight-mouthed silence, regretting the wasted sirs. When I got out I gave him a dollar tip to confuse him. Miranda paid the fare.

"I'd like to look at the bungalow," I told her in the lobby. "But first I want to talk to the switchboard operator."

"I'll get the key and wait for you."

The operator was a frozen virgin who dreamed about men at night and hated them in the daytime. "Yes?"

"Yesterday afternoon you had a call for a limousine from the Burbank airport."

"We do not answer questions of that nature."

"That wasn't a question. It was a statement."

"I'm very busy," she said. Her tone clicked like pennies; her eyes were small and hard and shiny like dimes.

I put a dollar bill on the desk by her elbow. She looked at it as if it was unclean. "I'll have to call the manager."

"All right. I work for Mr. Sampson."

"Mr. *Ralph* Sampson?" She lilted, she trilled.

"That's correct."

"But he was the one that made the call!"

"I know. What happened to it?"

"He canceled it almost immediately, before I had an opportunity to tell the driver. Did he have a change of plan?"

"Apparently. You're sure it was him both times?"

"Oh yes," she said. "I know Mr. Sampson well. He's been coming here for years."

She picked up the unclean dollar lest it contaminate her desk, and tucked it into a cheap plastic handbag. Then she turned to the switchboard, which had three red lights on it.

Miranda stood up when I came back to the lobby. It was hushed and rich, deep-carpeted, deep-chaired, with mauve-coated bellboys at attention. She moved like a live young nymph in a museum. "Ralph hasn't been here for nearly a month. I asked the assistant manager."

"Did he give you the key?"

"Of course. Alan's gone to open the bungalow."

I followed her down a corridor that ended in a wrought-iron door. The grounds back of the main building were laid out in little avenues, with bungalows on either side, set among terraced lawns and flower beds. They covered a city block, enclosed by high stone walls like a prison. But the prisoners of those walls could lead a very full life. There were tennis courts, a swimming pool, a restaurant, a bar, a night club. All they needed was a full wallet or a blank checkbook.

Sampson's bungalow was larger than most of the others and had more terrace. The door at the side was standing open. We passed through a hall cluttered with uncomfortable-looking Spanish chairs into a big room with a high oak-beamed ceiling.

On the chesterfield in front of the dead fireplace Taggert was hunched over a telephone directory. "I thought I'd call a buddy of mine." He looked up at Miranda with a half smile. "Since I have to hang around anyway."

"I thought you were going to stay with me." Her voice was high and uncertain.

"Did you?"

I looked around the room, which was mass-produced and impersonal like most hotel rooms. "Where does your father keep his private stuff?"

"In his room, I suppose. He doesn't keep much here. A few changes of clothes."

She showed me the door of the bedroom across the hall and switched on the light.

"What on earth has he done to it?" she said.

The room was twelve-sided and windowless. The indirect lights were red. The walls were covered with thick red stuff that hung in folds from the ceiling to the floor. A heavy arm-chair and the bed in the room's center were covered with the same dark red. The crowning touch was a circular mirror in the ceiling which repeated the room upside down. My memory struggled in the red gloom and found the comparison it wanted: a Neapolitan-type bordello I'd visited in Mexico City—on a case.

"No wonder he took to drink, if he had to sleep in here."

"It didn't used to be like this," she said. "He must have had it redone."

I moved around the room. Each of the twelve panels was embroidered in gold with one of the twelve signs of the zodiac—the archer, the bull, the twins, and the nine others.

"Is your father interested in astrology?"

"Yes, he is." She said it shamefacedly. "I've tried to argue with him, but it doesn't do any good. He went off the deep end when Bob died. I had no idea he'd gone so far in it, though."

"Does he go to a particular astrologist? The woods are full of them."

"I wouldn't know."

I found the entrance to the closet behind a movable curtain. It was stuffed with suits and shirts and shoes, from golf clothes to evening dress. I went through the pockets systematically. In the breast pocket of a jacket I found a wallet. The wallet contained a mass of twenties and a single photograph.

I held it up to the bulb that lit the closet. It was a sibylline face, with dark and mournful eyes and a full drooping mouth. On either side the black hair fell straight to the high neckline of a black dress that merged into artistic shadows at the bottom of the picture. A feminine hand had written in white ink across the shadows: "To Ralph from Fay with Blessings."

It was a face I should know. I remembered the melancholy eyes but nothing else. I replaced the wallet in Sampson's jacket and added the picture to my photographic collection of one.

"Look," Miranda said, when I stepped back into the room. She was lying on the bed with her skirt above her knees. Her body in the rosy light seemed to be burning. She closed her eyes. "What does this mad room make you think of?"

Her hair was burning all around the edges. Her upturned face was closed and dead. And her slender body was burning up, like a sacrifice on an altar.

I crossed the room and put my hand on her shoulder. The ruddy light shone through my hand and reminded me that I contained a skeleton. "Open your eyes."

She opened them smiling. "You saw it, didn't you? The sacrifice on the heathen altar—like Salammbô."

"You do read too many books," I said.

My hand was still on her shoulder, conscious of sunned flesh. She turned toward me and pulled me down. Her lips were hot on my face.

"What goes on?" Taggert asked, from the doorway. The red light on his face made him look choleric, but he was smiling his same half smile. The incident amused him.

I stood up and straightened my coat. I was not amused. Miranda was the freshest thing I'd touched in many a day. She made the blood run round in my veins like horses on a track.

"What's so hard in your coat pocket?" Miranda said distinctly.

"I'm wearing a gun."

I pulled out the dark woman's picture and showed it to both of them. "Did you ever see her before? She signs herself 'Fay.'"

"I never did," said Taggert.

"No," said Miranda. She was smiling at him side-eyed and secretly, as if she had won a point.

She'd been using me to stir him up, and it made me angry. The red room made me angry. It was like the inside of a sick brain, with no eyes to see out of, nothing to look at but the upside-down reflection of itself. I got out.

chapter **5**   *I pressed the bell, and in a minute a rich female voice gurgled in the speaking-tube. "Who is it, please?"*

"Lew Archer. Is Morris home?"

"Sure. Come on up." She sounded the buzzer that opened the inner door of the apartment lobby.

She was waiting when I reached the head of the stairs, a fat and fading blonde, happily married. "Long time no see." I winced, but she didn't notice. "Morris slept in this morning. He's still eating breakfast."

I glanced at my watch. It was three thirty. Morris Cramm was night legman for a columnist and worked from seven in the evening to five in the morning.

His wife led me through a living-room-bedroom combination crowded with papers and books and an unmade studio bed. Morris was at the kitchen table, in a bathrobe, staring down two fried eggs that were looking up at him. He was a dark little man with sharp black eyes behind thick spectacles. And behind the eyes was a card-index brain that contained the vital statistics of Los Angeles.

"Morning, Lew," he said, without getting up.

I sat down opposite him. "It's late afternoon."

"It's morning to me. Time is a relative concept. In summer when I go to bed the yellow sun shines overhead—Robert Louis Stevenson. Which lobe of my brain do you want to pick this morning?"

He italicized the last word, and Mrs. Cramm punctuated it by pouring me a cup of coffee. They half convinced me I had just got up after having a dream about the Sampsons. I wouldn't have minded being convinced that the Sampsons were a dream.

I showed him the picture signed "Fay." "Do you know the face? I have a hunch I've seen it before, and that could mean she's in pictures. She's a histrionic type."

He studied the piece of cardboard. "Superannuated vampire. Fortyish, but the picture's prewar, maybe ten years old. Fay Estabrook."

"You know her?"

He stabbed an egg and watched it bleed yellow on his plate. "I've seen her around. She was a star in the Pearl White era."

"What does she do for a living?"

"Nothing much. Lives quietly. She's been married once or twice." He overcame his reluctance and began to eat his eggs.

"Is she married now?"

"I wouldn't know. I don't think her last one took. She makes a little money doing bit parts. Sim Kuntz makes a place for her in his pictures. He was her director in the old days."

"She wouldn't be an astrologist on the side?"

"Could be." He jabbed viciously at his second egg. It humiliated him not to know the answer to a question. "I got no file on her, Lew. She isn't that important any more. But she must have some income. She makes a moderate splash. I've seen her at Chasen's."

"All by herself, no doubt."

He screwed up his small serious face, chewing sideways like a camel. "You're picking both lobes, you son of a gun. Do I get paid for wearying my lobes?"

"A fin," I said. "I'm on an expense account." Mrs. Cramm hovered breastily over me and poured me another cup of coffee.

"I've seen her more than once with an English-remittance-man type."

"Description?"

"White hair, premature, eyes blue or gray. Middle-sized and wiry. Well-dressed. Handsome if you like an aging chorus boy."

"You know I do. Anybody else?" I couldn't show him Sampson's picture or mention Sampson's name. He was paid for collecting names in groups of two. Very badly paid.

"Once at least. She had late supper with a fat tourist-type dressed in ten-dollar bills. He was so squiffed he had to be helped to the door. That was several months ago. I haven't seen her since."

"And you don't know where she lives?"

"Somewhere out of town. It's off my beat. Anyway, I've given you a fin's worth."

"I won't deny it, but there's one more thing. Is Simeon Kuntz working now?"

"He's doing an independent on the Telepictures lot. She might be out there. I heard they're shooting."

I handed him his bill. He kissed it and pretended to use it to light a cigarette. His wife snatched it out of his hand. When I left they were chasing each other around the kitchen, laughing like a couple of amiable maniacs.

My taxi was waiting in front of the apartment house. I took it home and went to work on the telephone directories for Los Angeles and environs. There was no Fay Estabrook listed.

I called Telepictures in Universal City and asked for Fay Estabrook. The operator didn't know if she was on the lot; she'd have to make inquiries. On a small lot it meant that Fay was definitely a has-been where pictures were concerned.

The operator came back to the telephone: "Miss Estabrook is here, but she's working just now. Is there a message?"

"I'll come out. What stage is she on?"

"Number three."

"Is Simeon Kuntz directing?"

"Yes. You have to have a pass, you know."

"I have," I lied.

Before I left I made the mistake of taking off my gun and hanging it away in the hall closet. Its harness was uncomfortable on a hot day, and I didn't expect to be using it. There was a bag of battered golf clubs in the closet. I took them out to the garage and slung them into the back of my car.

Universal City wore its stucco facades like yellowing paper collars. The Telepictures buildings were newer than the rest, but they didn't seem out of place among the rundown bars and seedy restaurants that lined the boulevard. Their plaster walls had a jerry-built look, as if they didn't expect to last.

I parked around the corner in a residential block and lugged my bag of clubs to the main entrance of the studio. There were ten or twelve people sitting on straight-backed chairs outside the casting-office, trying to look sought-after and complacent. A girl in a neat black suit brushed threadbare was taking off her gloves and putting them on. A grim-faced woman sat with a grim-faced little girl on her knee, dressed in pink silk and whining. The usual assortment of displaced actors—fat, thin, bearded, shaven, tuxedoed, sombreroed, sick, alcoholic, and senile—sat there with great dignity, waiting for nothing.

I tore myself away from all that glamour, and went down the dingy hall to the swinging gate. A middle-aged man with a chin like the butt end of a ham was sitting beside the gate in a blue guard's uniform, with a black visored cap on his head and a black holster on his hip. I stopped at the gate, hugging the golf bag as if it meant a great deal to me. The guard half opened his eyes and tried to place me.

Before he could say anything that might arouse his suspicions, I said: "Mr. Kuntz wants these right away."

The guards at the majors asked for passports and visas and did everything but probe the body cavities for concealed hand grenades. The independents were laxer, and I was taking a chance on that.

He pushed open the gate and waved me through. I emerged in a white-hot concrete alley like the entrance to a maze and lost myself among the anonymous buildings. I turned down a dirt road with a sign that said "Western Main Street," and went up to a couple of painters who were painting the weather-warped front of a saloon with a swinging door and no insides.

"Stage three?" I asked them.

"Turn right, then left at the first turn. You'll see the sign across the street from New York Tenement."

I turned right and passed London Street and Pioneer Log Cabin, then left in front of Continental Hotel. The false fronts looked so real from a distance, so ugly and thin close up, that they made me feel suspicious of my own reality. I felt like throwing away the golf bag and going into Continental Hotel for an imitation drink with the other ghosts. But ghosts had no glands, and I was sweating freely. I should have brought something lighter, like a badminton racquet.

When I reached stage three the red light was burning and the soundproof doors were shut. I set the golf bag down against the wall and waited. After a while the light went out. The door opened, and a herd of chorus girls in bunny costumes came out and wandered up the street. I held the door for the last pair and stepped inside.

The interior of the sound stage was a reproduction of a theater, with red plush orchestra seats and boxes, and gilt rococo decorations. The orchestra pit was empty and the stage was bare, but there was a small audience grouped in the first few rows. A young man in shirt sleeves was adjusting an overhead baby spot. He called for lights, and the baby spot illuminated the head of a woman sitting in the center of the first row facing a camera. I moved down the side aisle and recognized Fay before the light went out.

The light came on again, a buzzer sounded, and there was a heavy silence in the room. It was broken by the woman's deep voice:

"Isn't he marvelous?"

She turned to a gray-mustached man beside her and gently shook his arm. He smiled and nodded.

"Cut!" A tired-looking little man with a bald head, beautifully clothed in pale-blue gabardines, got up from behind the camera and leaned toward Fay Estabrook. "Look, Fay, you're his mother. He's up there on the stage singing his heart out for you. This is his first big chance; it's what you've hoped and prayed for all these years."

His emotional central European voice was so compelling that I glanced at the stage involuntarily. It was still empty.

"Isn't he marvelous?" the woman said strenuously.

"Better. Better. But remember the question is not a real question. It is a rhetorical question. The accent is on the 'marvelous.' "

"Isn't he marvelous!" the woman cried.

"More accent. More heart, my dear Fay. Pour out your mother love to your son singing so gloriously up there behind the footlights. Try again."

"Isn't he marvelous!" the woman yelped viciously.

"No! Sophistication is not the line. You must keep your intelligence out of this. Simplicity. Warm, loving simplicity. Do you get it, my dear Fay?"

She looked angry and distraught. Everyone in the room, from assistant director to prop man, was watching her expectantly. "Isn't he marvelous?" she said throatily.

"Much, much better," said the little man. He called for lights and camera.

"Isn't he marvelous?" she said again. The gray-mustached man smiled and nodded some more. He put his hand over hers, and they smiled into each others' eyes.

"Cut!"

The smiles faded into weary boredom. The lights went out. The little director called for number seventy-seven. "You may go, Fay. Tomorrow at eight. And try to get a good night's sleep, darling." The way he said it sounded very unpleasant.

She didn't answer. While a new group of actors was forming in the wings of the theater stage and a camera rolled toward them, she rose and walked up the central aisle. I followed her out of the gloomy warehouse-like building into the sun.

I stood in the doorway as she walked away, not quickly, with movements a little random and purposeless. In her dowdy costume—black hat with a widow's veil and plain black coat—her big, handsome body looked awkward and ungainly. It may have been the sun in my eyes or simple romanticism, but I had the feeling that the evil which hung in studio air like an odorless gas was concentrated in that heavy black figure wandering up the empty factitious street.

When she was out of sight around the Continental Hotel corner, I picked up the golf bag and followed her. I started to sweat again, and I felt like an aging caddy, the kind that never quite became a pro.

She had joined a group of half a dozen women of all ages and shapes which was headed for the main entrance. Before they got there, they turned off into an alley. I trotted after them and saw them disappearing under a stucco arch labeled "Dressing Rooms."

I pushed open the swinging gate beside the guard and started out. He remembered me and the golf clubs:

"Didn't he want them?"

"He's going to play badminton instead."

chapter **6**   I was waiting when she came out,
parked with my motor idling at a yellow curb near the en-
trance. She turned up the sidewalk in the other direction.
She had changed to a well-cut dark suit, a small slanted hat.
Will or foundation garments had drawn her body erect.
From the rear she looked ten years younger.

Half a block from me she stopped by a black sedan, unlocked it and got in. I eased out into the traffic and let her
slide into the lane ahead of me. The sedan was a new Buick.
I wasn't concerned about her noticing my car. Los Angeles
County was crawling with blue convertibles, and the traffic
on the boulevard was a kaleidoscope being shaken.

She added her personal touch to the pattern, cutting in
and out of lanes, driving furiously and well. In the overpass
I had to touch seventy to keep her in sight. I didn't think
she was aware of me; she was doing it for fun. She went down
Sunset at a steady fifty, headed for the sea. Fifty-five and
sixty on the curves in Beverly Hills. Her heavy car was burning rubber. In my lighter car I was gambling at even odds with
centrifugal force. My tires screeched and shuddered.

On the long, looping final grade sloping down to Pacific
Palisades I let her go away from me and almost lost her. I
caught her again in the straightaway a minute before she
turned off the boulevard to the right.

I followed her up a road marked "Woodlawn Lane," which
wound along the hillside. A hundred yards ahead of me as I
came out of a curve she swung wide and turned into a driveway. I stopped my car where I was and parked under a
eucalyptus tree.

Through the japonica hedge that lined the sidewalk I saw her climb the steps to the door of a white house. She unlocked it and went in. The house was two-storied, set far back from the street among trees, with an attached garage built into the side of the hill. It was a handsome house for a woman on her way out.

After a while I got tired of watching the unopening door. I took off my coat and tie, folded them over the back of the seat, and rolled up my sleeves. There was a long-spouted oil-can in the trunk, and I took it with me. I walked straight up the driveway past the Buick and into the open door of the garage.

The garage was enormous, big enough to hold a two-ton truck with space for the Buick to spare. The queer thing was that it looked as if a heavy truck had recently been there. There were wide tire marks on the concrete floor, and thick oil drippings.

A small window high in the rear wall of the garage looked out on the back yard just above the level of the ground. A heavy-shouldered man in a scarlet silk sport shirt was sitting in a canvas deck chair with his back to me. His short hair looked thicker and blacker than Ralph Sampson's should have. I raised myself on my toes and pressed my face against the glass. Even through its dingy surface the scene was as vivid as paint: the broad, unconscious back of the man in the scarlet shirt, the brown bottle of beer and the bowl of salted peanuts in the grass beside him, the orange tree over his head hung with unripe oranges like dark-green golf balls.

He leaned sideways, the crooked fingers of his large hand groping for the bowl of peanuts. The hand missed the bowl and scrabbled in the grass like a crippled lobster. Then he turned his head, and I saw the side of his face. It wasn't Ralph Sampson's, and it wasn't the face the man in the scarlet shirt had started out with. It was a stone face hacked out by a primitive sculptor. It told a very common twentieth-century story: too many fights, too many animal guts, not enough brains.

I returned to the tire marks and went down on my knees to examine them. Too late to do anything but stay where I was, I heard the shuffling footsteps on the driveway.

The man in the scarlet shirt said from the door: "What business you got messing around in here? You got no business messing around in here."

I inverted the oilcan and squirted a stream of oil at the wall. "Get out of my light, please."

"What's that?" he said laboriously. His upper lip was puffed thick as a mouth guard.

He was no taller than I was, and he wasn't as wide as the door, but he gave that impression. He made me nervous, the way you feel talking to a strange bulldog on his master's property. I stood up.

"Yes," I said. "You certainly got them, brother."

I didn't like the way he moved toward me. His left shoulder was forward and his chin in, as if every hour of his day was divided into twenty three-minute rounds.

"What do you mean, we got them? We ain't got nothing, but you get yourself some trouble you come selling your woof around here."

"Termites," I said rapidly. He was close enough to let me smell his breath. Beer and salted peanuts and bad teeth. "You tell Mrs. Goldsmith she's got them for sure."

"Termites?" He was flat on his heels. I could have knocked him down, but he wouldn't have stayed down.

"The tiny animals that eat wood." I squirted more oil at the wall. "The little muckers."

"What you got in that there can? That there can."

"This here can?"

"Yeah." I'd established rapport.

"It's termite-killer," I said. "They eat it and they die. You tell Mrs. Goldsmith she's got them all right."

"I don't know no Mrs. Goldsmith."

"The lady of the house. She called up headquarters for an inspection."

"Headquarters?" he said suspiciously. His scar-tissue-padded brows descended over his little empty eyes like shutters.

"Termite-control headquarters. Killabug is termite-control headquarters for the Southern California area."

"Oh!" He was puzzling over the words. "Yeah. But we got no Mrs. Goldsmith here."

"Isn't this Eucalyptus Lane?"

"Naw, this is Woodlawn Lane. You got the wrong address, bud."

"I'm awfully sorry," I said. "I thought this was Eucalyptus Lane."

"Naw, Woodlawn." He smiled widely at my ridiculous mistake.

"I better be going then. Mrs. Goldsmith will be looking for me."

"Yeah. Only wait a minute."

His left hand came out fast and took me by the collar. He cocked his right. "Don't come messing around in here any more. You got no business messing around in here."

His face filled out with angry blood. His eyes were hot and wild. There was a bright seepage of saliva at the cracked and folded corners of his mouth. A punchy fighter was less predictable than a bulldog, and twice as dangerous.

"Look." I raised the can. "This stuff will blind you."

I squirted oil in his eyes. He let out a howl of imaginary agony. I jerked sideways. His right went by my ear and left it burning. My shirt collar ripped loose and dangled from his clenched hand. He spread his right hand over his oil-doused eyes and moaned like a baby. Blindness was the one thing he feared.

A door opened behind me when I was halfway down the drive, but I didn't show my face by looking back. I ducked around the corner of the hedge and kept running, away from my car. I circled the block on foot.

When I came back to the convertible the road was deserted. The garage doors were closed, but the Buick was still standing in the drive. The white house among its trees looked very peaceful and innocent in the early evening light.

It was nearly dark when the lady of the house came out in a spotted ocelot coat. I passed the entrance to the drive before the Buick backed out, and waited for it on Sunset Boulevard. She drove with greater fury and less accuracy all the way back to Hollywood, through Westwood, Bel-Air, Beverley Hills. I kept her in sight.

Near the corner of Hollywood and Vine, where everything ends and a great many things begin, she turned into a private parking lot and left her car. I double-parked in the street till I saw her enter Swift's, a gaudy figure walking like a slightly elated lady. Then I went home and changed my shirt.

The gun in my closet tempted me, but I didn't put it on. I compromised by taking it out of the holster and putting it in the glove compartment of my car.

chapter **7**   *The back room of Swift's was paneled in black oak that glowed dimly under the polished brass chandeliers. It was lined on two sides with leather-cushioned booths. The rest of the floor space was covered with tables. All of the booths and most of the tables were crowded with highly dressed people eating or waiting to be fed. Most of the women were tight-skinned, starved too thin for their bones. Most of the men had the masculine Hollywood look, which was harder to describe. An insistent self-consciousness in their loud words and wide gestures, as if God had a million-dollar contract to keep an eye on them.*

Fay Estabrook was in a back booth, with a blue flannel elbow on the table opposite her. The rest of her companion was hidden by the partition.

I went to the bar against the third wall and ordered a beer. "Bass ale, Black Horse, Carta Blanca, or Guinness stout? We don't serve domestic beer after six o'clock."

I ordered Bass, gave the bartender a dollar and told him to keep the change. There wasn't any change. He went away.

I leaned forward to look in the mirror behind the bar and caught a three-quarters view of Fay Estabrook's face. It was earnest and intense. The mouth was moving rapidly. Just then the man stood up.

He was the kind who was usually in the company of

younger women, the neat and ageless kind who turned a
dollar year after year at nobody knew what. He was the aging
chorus boy Cramm had described. His blue jacket fitted him
too well. A white silk scarf at his throat set off his silver hair.

He was shaking hands with a red-haired man who was
standing by the booth. I recognized the red-haired man when
he turned and wandered back to his own table in the center
of the room. He was a contract writer for Metro named Russell Hunt.

The silver-haired man waved good-bye to Fay Estabrook
and set his course for the door. I watched him in the mirror.
He walked efficiently and neatly, looking straight ahead as if
the place was deserted. As far as he was concerned it was deserted. Nobody lifted a hand or raised a lip over teeth. When
he went out a few heads turned, a couple of eyebrows were
elevated. Fay Estabrook was left in her booth by herself as
if she had caught his infection and could communicate it.

I carried my glass to Russell Hunt's table. He was sitting
with a fat man who had a round ugly nose turned up at the
tip and bright little agent's eyes.

"How's the word business, Russell?"

"Hello, Lew."

He wasn't glad to see me. I earned three hundred a week
when I was working, and that made me one of the peasantry.
He made fifteen hundred. An ex-reporter from Chicago who
had sold his first novel to Metro and never written another,
Hunt was turning from a hopeful kid to a nasty old man with
the migraine and a swimming pool he couldn't use because
he was afraid of the water. I had helped him lose his second
wife to make way for his third, who was no improvement.

"Sit down, sit down," he said, when I didn't go away.

"Have a drink. It dissipates the megrims. I do not drink to dissipate myself. I dissipate the megrims."

"Hold it," said agent eyes. "If you're a creative artist you may sit down. Otherwise I can hardly be expected to waste my time with you."

"Timothy is my agent," Russell said. "I am the goose that lays his golden eggs. Observe his nervous fingers toying with the steak knife, his eyes fastened wistfully upon my rounded throat. Boding me no good, I ween."

"He weens," said Timothy. "Do you create?"

I slid into the patois and a chair. "I am a man of action. A sleuth hound, to wit."

"Lew's a detective," Russell said. "He unearths people's guilty secrets and exposes them to the eyes of a scandalized world."

"Now, how low can you get?" asked Timothy cheerfully.

I didn't like the crack, but I'd come for information, not exercise. He saw the look on my face and turned to the waiter who was standing by his chair.

"Who was that you were shaking hands with?" I asked Russell.

"The elegant lad in the scarf? Fay said his name was Troy. They were married at one time, so she ought to know."

"What does he do?"

"I wouldn't know for sure. I've seen him around: Palm Springs, Las Vegas, Tia Juana."

"Las Vegas?"

"I think so. Fay says he's an importer, but if he's an importer I'm a monkey's uncle." He remembered his role. "Curiously enough, I am a monkey's uncle, though I must confess that no one was more surprised than I when my younger sister, the one with the three breasts, gave birth last Whitsuntide to the cutest little chimpanzee you ever did see. She was Lady Greystoke by her first marriage, you know."

His patter ceased abruptly. His face became grim and miserable again. "Another drink," he said to the waiter. "A double Scotch. Make it the same all round."

"Just a minute, sir." The waiter was a wizened old man with black thumbtack eyes. "I'm taking this gentleman's order."

"He won't serve me." Russell flung out his arms in a burlesque gesture of despair. "I'm eighty-six again."

The waiter pretended to be absorbed in what Timothy was saying.

"But I don't want French fried potatoes. I want au gratin potatoes."

"We don't have au gratin, sir."

"You can make them, can't you?" Timothy said, his retroussé nostrils glaring.

"Thirty-five or forty minutes, sir."

"O God!" Timothy said. "What kind of a beanery is this? Let's go to Chasen's, Russell. I got to have au gratin potatoes."

The waiter stood watching him as if from a great distance. I glanced around him and saw that Fay Estabrook was still at her table, working on a bottle of wine.

"They don't let me into Chasen's any more," Russell said. "On account of I am an agent of the Cominform. I wrote a movie with a Nazi for a villain, so I am an agent of the Cominform. That's where my money comes from, friends. It's tainted Moscow gold."

"Cut it out," I said. "Do you know Fay Estabrook?"

"A little. I passed her on the way up a few years ago. A few more years, and I'll pass her on the way down."

"Introduce me to her."

"Why?"

"I've always wanted to meet her."

"I don't get it, Lew. She's old enough to be your wife."

I said in language he could understand: "I have a sentimental regard for her, stemming from the dear dead days beyond recall."

"Introduce him if he wants," said Timothy. "Sleuth hounds make me nervous. Then I can eat my au gratin potatoes in peace."

Russell got up laboriously, as if the top of his red head supported the ceiling.

"Good night," I said to Timothy. "Have fun with the hired help before they throw you out on your fat neck."

I picked up my drink and steered Russell across the room. "Don't tell her my business," I said in his ear.

"Who am I to wash your dirty linen in public? In private it's another matter. I'd love to wash your dirty linen in private. It's a fetish with me."

"I throw it away when it's dirty."

"But what a waste. Please save it for me in future. Just send it to me care of Kraft-Ebing at the clinic."

Mrs. Estabrook looked up at us with eyes like dark searchlights.

"This is Lew Archer, Fay. The agent. Of the Communist International, that is. He's an old admirer of yours in his secret heart."

"How nice!" she said, in a voice that was wasted on mother roles. "Won't you sit down?"

"Thank you." I sat down in the leather seat opposite her.

"Excuse me," Russell said. "I have to look after Timothy. He's waging a class war with the waiter. Tomorrow night it's his turn to look after me. Oh goody!" He went away, lost in his private maze of words.

"It's nice to be remembered occasionally," the woman said. "Most of my friends are gone, and all of them are forgotten. Helene and Florence and Mae—all of them gone and forgotten."

Her winy sentimentality, half phony and half real, was a pleasant change in a way from Russell's desperate double talk. I took my cue.

"*Sic transit gloria mundi.* Helene Chadwick was a great player in her day. But you're still carrying on."

"I try to keep my hand in, Archer. The life has gone out of the town, though. We used to care about picture-making— really care. I made three grand a week at my peak, but it wasn't the money we worked for."

"The play's the thing." It was less embarrassing to quote.

"The play *was* the thing. It isn't like that any more. The town has lost its sincerity. No life left in it. No life left in either it or I."

She poured the final ounce from her half bottle of sherry and drank it down in one long mournful swallow. I nursed my drink.

"You're doing all right." I let my glance slide down the heavy body half revealed by the open fur coat. It was good for her age, tight-waisted, high-bosomed, with amphora hips. And it was alive, with a subtly persistent female power, an animal pride like a cat's.

"I like you, Archer. You're sympathetic. Tell me, when were you born?"

"What year, you mean?"

"The date."

"The second of June."

"Really? I didn't expect you to be Geminian. Geminis have no heart. They're double-souled like the Twins, and they lead a double life. Are you cold-hearted, Archer?"

She leaned toward me with wide, unfocused eyes. I couldn't tell whether she was kidding me or herself.

"I'm everybody's friend," I said, to break the spell. "Children and dogs adore me. I raise flowers and have green thumbs."

"You're a cynic," she answered sulkily. "I thought you were going to be sympathetic, but you're in the Air triplicity and I'm in the Water."

"We'd make a wonderful air-sea rescue team."

She smiled and said chidingly: "Don't you believe in the stars?"

"Do you?"

"Of course I do—in a purely scientific way. When you look at the evidence, you simply can't deny it. I'm Cancer, for example, and anybody can see that I'm the Cancer type. I'm sensitive and imaginative; I can't do without love. The people I love can twist me around their little finger, but I can be stubborn when I have to be. I've been unlucky in marriage, like so many other Cancerians. Are you married, Archer?"

"Not now."

"That means you were. You'll marry again. Gemini always

does. And he often marries a woman older than himself, did you know that?"

"No." Her insistent voice was pushing me slightly off balance, threatening to dominate the conversation and me. "You're very convincing," I said.

"What I'm telling you is the truth."

"You should do it professionally. There's money in it for a smooth operator with a convincing spiel."

Her candid eyes narrowed to two dark slits like peepholes in a fort. She studied me through them, made a tactical decision, and opened them wide again. They were dark pools of innocence, like poisoned wells.

"Oh, no," she said. "I never do this professionally. It's a talent I have, a gift—Cancer is frequently psychic—and I feel it's my duty to use it. But not for money—only for my friends."

"You're lucky to have an independent income."

Her thin-stemmed glass twirled out of her fingers and broke in two pieces on the table. "That's Gemini for you," she said. "Always looking for facts."

I felt a slight twinge of doubt and shrugged it off. She'd fired at random and hit the target by accident. "I didn't mean to be curious," I said.

"Oh, I know that." She rose suddenly, and I felt the weight of her body standing over me. "Let's get out of here, Archer. I'm starting to drop things again. Let's go some place we can talk."

"Why not?"

She left an unbroken bill on the table and walked out with heavy dignity. I followed her, pleased with my startling success but feeling a little like a male spider about to be eaten by a female spider.

Russell was at his table with his head in his arms. Timothy was yelping at the captain of waiters like a terrier who has cornered some small defenseless animal. The captain of waiters was explaining that the au gratin potatoes would be ready in fifteen minutes.

chapter **8**   In the Hollywood Roosevelt bar she complained of the air and said she felt wretched and old. Nonsense, I told her, but we moved to the Zebra Room. She had shifted to Irish whisky, which she drank straight. In the Zebra Room she accused a man at the next table of looking at her contemptuously. I suggested more air. She drove down Wilshire as if she was trying to break through into another dimension. I had to park the Buick for her at the Ambassador. I'd left my car at Swift's.

She quarreled with the Ambassador barman on the grounds that he laughed at her when he turned his back. I took her to the downstairs bar at the Huntoon Park, which wasn't often crowded. Wherever we went, there were people who recognized her, but nobody joined us or stood up. Not even the waiters made a fuss over her. She was on her way out.

Except for a couple leaning together at the other end of the bar, the Huntoon Park was deserted. The thickly carpeted, softly lighted basement was a funeral parlor where the evening we had killed was laid out. Mrs. Estabrook was pale as a corpse, but she was vertical, able to see, talk, drink, and possibly even think.

I was steering her in the direction of the Valerio, hoping that she'd name it. A few more drinks, and I could take the risk of suggesting it myself. I was drinking with her, but not enough to affect me. I made inane conversation, and she didn't notice the difference. I was waiting. I wanted her far enough gone to say whatever came into her head. Archer the heavenly twin and midwife to oblivion.

I looked at my face in the mirror behind the bar and didn't like it too well. It was getting thin and predatory-looking. My nose was too narrow, my ears were too close to my head. My eyelids were the kind that overlapped at the outside corners and made my eyes look triangular in a way that I usually liked. Tonight my eyes were like tiny stone wedges hammered between the lids.

She leaned forward over the bar with her chin in her hands, looking straight down into her half-empty liqueur glass. The pride that had kept her body erect and organized her face had seeped away. She was hunched there tasting the bitterness at the bottom of her life, droning out elegies:

"He never took care of himself, but he had the body of a wrestler and the head of an Indian chief. He was part Indian. Nothing mean about him, though. One sweet guy. Quiet and easy, never talked much. But passionate, and a real one-woman man, the last I ever seen. He got T.B. and went off in one summer. It broke me up. I never got over it since. He was the only man I ever loved."

"What did you say his name was?"

"Bill." She looked at me slyly. "I didn't say. He was my foreman. I had one of the first big places in the valley. We were together for a year, and then he died. That was twenty-five years ago, and I been feeling ever since I might as well be dead myself."

She raised her large tearless eyes and met my glance in the mirror. I wanted to respond to her melancholy look, but I didn't know what to do with my face.

I tried smiling to encourage myself. I was a good Joe after all. Consorter with roughnecks, tarts, hard cases and easy marks; private eye at the keyhole of illicit bedrooms; informer to jealousy, rat behind the walls, hired gun to anybody with fifty dollars a day; but a good Joe after all. The wrinkles formed at the corner of my eyes, the wings of my nose; the lips drew back from the teeth, but there was no smile. All I got was a lean famished look like a coyote's sneer. The face had seen too many bars, too many rundown hotels and crummy love nests, too many courtrooms and prisons, post-mortems and police lineups, too many nerve ends showing like tortured worms. If I found the face on a stranger, I wouldn't trust it. I caught myself wondering how it looked to Miranda Sampson.

"To hell with the three-day parties," Mrs. Estabrook said. "To hell with the horses and the emeralds and the boats. One good friend is better than any of them, and I haven't got one good friend. Sim Kuntz said he was my friend, and he tells me I'm making my last picture. I lived my life twenty-five years ago, and I'm all washed up. You don't want to get mixed up with me, Archer."

She was right. Still, I was interested, apart from my job. She'd had a long journey down from a high place, and she knew what suffering was. Her voice had dropped its phony correctness and the other things she had learned from studio coaches. It was coarse and pleasantly harsh. It placed her childhood in Detroit or Chicago or Indianapolis, at the beginning of the century, on the wrong side of town.

She drained her glass and stood up. "Take me home, Archer."

I slid off my stool with gigolo alacrity and took her by the arm. "You can't go home like this. You need another drink to snap you back."

"You're nice." My skin was thin enough to feel the irony. "Only I can't take this place. It's a morgue. For Christ's sake," she yelled at the bartender, "where are all the merrymakers?"

"Aren't you a merrymaker, madam?"

I pulled her away from the start of another quarrel, up the steps and out. There was a light fog in the air, blurring the neons. Above the tops of the buildings the starless sky was dull and low. She shivered, and I felt the tremor in her arm.

"There's a good bar next street up," I said.

"The Valerio?"

"I think that's it."

"All right. One more drink, then I got to go home."

I opened the door of her car and helped her in. Her breast leaned against my shoulder heavily. I moved back. I preferred a less complicated kind of pillow, stuffed with feathers, not memories and frustrations.

The waitress in the Valerio cantina called her by name, escorted us to a booth, emptied the empty ash tray. The bartender, a smooth-faced young Greek, came all the way around from behind the bar to say hello to her and to ask after Mr. Sampson.

"He's still in Nevada," she said. I was watching her face,

and she caught my look. "A very good friend of mine. He stops here when he's in town."

The two-block ride, or her welcome, had done her good. She was almost sprightly. Maybe I'd made a mistake.

"A great old guy," the bartender said. "We miss him around here."

"Ralph's a wonderful, wonderful man," said Mrs. Estabrook. "One sweet guy."

The bartender took our order and went away.

"Have you cast his horoscope?" I said. "This friend of yours?"

"Now, how did you know? He's Capricorn. One sweet guy, but a very dominant type. He's had tragedy in his life, though. His only boy was killed in the war. Ralph's sun was squared by Uranus, you see. You wouldn't know what that can mean to a Capricornian."

"No. Does it mean much to him?"

"Yes, it does. Ralph has been developing his spiritual side. Uranus is against him, but the other planets are with him. It's given him courage to know that." She leaned toward me confidentially. "I wish I could show you the room I redecorated for him. It's in one of the bungalows here, but they wouldn't let us in."

"Is he staying here now?"

"No, he's in Nevada. He has a very lovely home on the desert."

"Ever been there?"

"You ask so many questions." She smiled side-eyed in ghastly coquetry. "You wouldn't be getting jealous?"

"You told me you had no friends."

"Did I say that? I was forgetting Ralph."

The bartender brought our drinks, and I sipped mine. I was facing the back of the room. A door in the wall beside the silent grand piano opened into the Valerio lobby. Alan Taggert and Miranda came through the door together.

"Excuse me," I said to Mrs. Estabrook.

Miranda saw me when I stood up, and started forward. I put a finger to my mouth and waved her back with the other hand. She moved away with a wide-mouthed, bewildered look.

Alan was quicker. He took her arm and hustled her out the door. I followed them. The bartender was mixing a drink. The waitress was serving a customer. Mrs. Estabrook hadn't looked up. The door closed behind me.

Miranda turned on me. "I don't understand this. You're supposed to be looking for Ralph."

"I'm working on a contact. Go away, please."

"But I've been trying to get in touch with you." She was strained to the point of tears.

I said to Taggert: "Take her away before she spoils my night's work. Out of the city, if possible." Three hours of Fay had sharpened my temper.

"But Mrs. Sampson's been phoning for you," he said.

A Filipino bellboy was standing against the wall hearing everything we said. I took them around the corner into the half-lit lobby. "What about?"

"She's heard from Ralph." Miranda's eyes glowed amber like a deer's. "A special-delivery letter. He wants her to send him money. Not send it exactly, but have it ready for him."

"How much money?"

"A hundred thousand dollars."

"Say that again."

"He wants her to cash a hundred thousand dollars' worth of bonds."

"Does she have that much?"

"She hasn't, but she can get it. Bert Graves has Ralph's power of attorney."

"What's she supposed to do with the money?"

"He said we'll hear from him again or he'll send a messenger for it."

"You're sure the letter's from him?"

"Elaine says it's in his writing."

"Does he say where he is?"

"No, but the letter's postmarked Santa Maria. He must have been there today."

"Not necessarily. What does Mrs. Sampson want me to do?"

"She didn't say. I suppose she wants your advice."

"All right, this is it. Tell her to have the money ready, but not to hand it over to anybody without proof that your father's alive."

"You think he's dead?" Her hand plucked at the neckline of her dress.

"I can't afford to guess." I turned to Taggert. "Can you fly Miranda up tonight?"

"I just phoned Santa Teresa. The airport's fogged in. First thing in the morning, though."

"Then tell her over the phone. I have a possible lead and I'm following it up. Graves had better contact the police, quietly. The local police and the Los Angeles police. And the F.B.I."

"The F.B.I.?" Miranda whispered.

"Yes," I said. "Kidnapping is a federal offense."

chapter **9**   When I went back to the bar, a young
Mexican in a tuxedo was leaning against the piano with a
guitar. His small tenor, plaintive and remote, was singing a
Spanish bullfighting song. His fingers marched thunderously
in the strings. Mrs. Estabrook was watching him and barely
noticed me when I sat down.

She clapped loudly when the song was finished, and beck-
oned him to our booth. "Bábalu. Pretty please." She handed
him a dollar.

He bowed and smiled, and returned to his singing.

"It's Ralph's favorite song," she said. "Domingo sings it
so well. He's got real Spanish blood in his veins."

"About this friend of yours, Ralph."

"What about him?"

"He wouldn't object to your being here with me?"

"Don't be silly. I want you to meet him some time. I know
you'll like him."

"What does he do?"

"He's more or less retired. He's got money."

"Why don't you marry him?"

She laughed harshly. "Didn't I tell you I had a husband?
But you don't have to worry about him. It's purely a business
proposition."

"I didn't know you were in business."

"Did I say I was in business?" She laughed again, much
too alertly, and changed the subject: "It's funny you suggesting I should marry Ralph. We're both married to other
people. Anyway, our friendship is on a different level. You
know, more spiritual."

She was sobering up on me. I raised my glass. "To friendship. On a different level."

While she was still drinking, I held up two fingers to the waitress. The second drink fixed her.

Her face went to pieces as if by its own weight. Her eyes went dull and unblinking. Her mouth hung open in a fixed yawn, the scarlet lips contrasting with the pink-and-white interior. She brought it together numbly and whispered: "I don't feel so good."

"I'll take you home."

"You're nice."

I helped her to her feet. The waitress held the door open, with a condoling smile for Mrs. Estabrook and a sharp glance at me. Mrs. Estabrook stumbled across the sidewalk like an old woman leaning on a cane that wasn't there. I held her up on her anesthetized legs, and we made it to the car.

Getting her in was like loading a sack of coal. Her head rolled into the corner between the door and the back of the seat. I started the car and headed for Pacific Palisades.

The motion of the car revived her after a while. "Got to get home," she said dully. "You know where I live?"

"You told me."

"Got to climb on the treadmill in the morning. Crap! I should weep if he throws me out of pictures. I got independent means."

"You look like a businesswoman," I said encouragingly.

"You're nice, Archer." The line was beginning to get me down. "Taking care of an old hag like me. You wouldn't like me if I told you where I got my money."

"Try me."

"But I'm not telling you." Her laugh was ugly and loose,

in a low register. I thought I caught overtones of mockery in it, but they may have been in my head. "You're too nice a boy."

Yeah, I said to myself, a clean-cut American type. Always willing to lend a hand to help a lady fall flat on her face in the gutter.

The lady passed out again. At least she said nothing more. It was a lonely drive down the midnight boulevard with her half-conscious body. In the spotted coat it was like a sleeping animal beside me in the seat, a leopard or a wildcat heavy with age. It wasn't really old—fifty at most—but it was full of the years, full and fermenting with bad memories. She'd told me a number of things about herself, but not what I wanted to know, and I was too sick of her to probe deeper. The one sure thing I knew about her she hadn't had to tell me: she was bad company for Sampson or any incautious man. Her playmates were dangerous—one rough, one smooth. And if anything had happened to Sampson she'd know it or find out.

She was awake when I parked in front of her house. "Put the car in the drive. Would you, honey?"

I backed across the road and took the car up the driveway. She needed help to climb the steps to the door, and handed me the key to open it. "You come in. I been trying to think of something I want to drink."

"You're sure it's all right? Your husband?"

Laughter growled in her throat. "We haven't lived together for years."

I followed her into the hallway. It was thick with darkness and her two odors, musk and alcohol, half animal and half human. I felt slippery waxed floor under my feet and wondered if she'd fall. She moved in her own house with the blind accuracy of a sleepwalker. I felt my way after her into a room to the left, where she switched on a lamp.

The room it brought out of darkness was nothing like the insane red room she had made for Ralph Sampson. It was big and cheerful even at night behind closed Venetian blinds. A solid middle-class room with post-Impressionist reproductions on the walls, built-in bookshelves, books on them, a radio-phonograph and a record cabinet, a glazed brick fireplace with a heavy sectional chesterfield curved in front of it. The only strangeness was in the pattern of the cloth that covered the chesterfield and the armchair under the lamp: brilliant green tropical plants against a white desert sky, with single eyes staring between the fronds. The pattern changed as I looked at it. The eyes disappeared and reappeared again. I sat down on a batch of them.

She was at the portable bar in the corner beside the fireplace. "What are you drinking?"

"Whisky and water."

She brought me my glass. Half of its contents slopped out en route, leaving a trail of dark splotches across the light-green carpet. She sat down beside me, depressing the cushioned seat. Her dark head swayed toward my shoulder and lodged there. I could see the few iron-gray strands the hairdresser had left in her hair so it wouldn't look dyed.

"I can't think of anything I want to drink," she whined. "Don't let me fall."

I put one arm around her shoulders, which were almost as wide as mine. She leaned hard against me. I felt the stir and swell of her breathing, gradually slowing down.

"Don't try to do anything to me, honey, I'm dead tonight.

Some other night. . . ." Her voice was soft and somehow girlish, but blurred. Blurred like the submarine glints of youth in her eyes.

Her eyes closed. I could see the faint tremor of her heart-beat in the veins of her withering eyelids. Their fringe of curved dark lashes was a vestige of youth and beauty which made her ruin seem final and hard. It was easier to feel sorry for her when she was sleeping.

To make certain that she was, I gently raised one of her eye-lids. The marbled eyeball stared whitely at nothing. I took away my arm and let her body subside on the cushions. Her breasts hung askew. Her stockings were twisted. She began to snore.

I went into the next room, closed the door behind me, and turned on the light. It shone down from the ceiling on a bleached mahogany refectory table with artificial flowers in the center, a china cabinet at one side, a built-in buffet at the other, six heavy chairs ranged around the wall on their haunches. I turned the light off and went into the kitchen, which was neat and well equipped.

I wondered for an instant if I had misjudged the woman. There were honest astrologists—and plenty of harmless drunks. Her house was like a hundred thousand others in Los Angeles County, almost too typical to be true. Except for the huge garage and the bulldog that guarded it.

The bathroom had walls of pastel-blue tile and a square blue tub. The cabinet over the sink was stuffed and heaped with tonics and patent medicines, creams and paints and powders, luminol, nembutal, veronal. The hypochondriac bottles and boxes overflowed on the back of the sink, the laundry hamper, and the toilet top. The clothes in the hamper were female. There was only one toothbrush in the holder. A razor but no shaving cream, nor any other trace of a man.

The bedroom next to the bathroom was flowered and prettied in pink like a prewar sentimental hope. There was a book on the stars on the bedside table. The clothes in the closet were women's, and there were a great many of them, with Saks and Magnin labels. The undergarments and night-clothes in the chest of drawers were peach and baby blue and black lace.

I looked under the twisted mass of stockings in the second drawer and found the core of strangeness in the house. It was a row of narrow packages held together with elastic bands. The packages contained money, all in bills, ones and fives and tens. Most of the bills were old and greasy. If all the packages assayed like the one I examined, the bottom of the drawer was lined with eight or ten thousand dollars.

I sat on my heels and looked at all that money. A bedroom drawer was hardly a good place to keep it. But it was safer than a bank for people who couldn't declare their income.

The burring ring of a telephone cut the silence like a dentist's drill. It struck a nerve, and I jumped. But I shut the drawer before I went into the hall where the telephone was. There was no sound from the woman in the living-room.

I muffled my voice with my tie. "Hello."

"Mr. Troy?" It was a woman.

"Yes."

"Is Fay there?" Her speech was rapid and clipped. "This is Betty."

"No."

"Listen, Mr. Troy. Fay was fried in the Valerio about an hour ago. The man she was with could be plain-clothes. He said he was taking her home. You wouldn't want him around when the truck goes through. And you know Fay when she's oiled."

"Yes," I said, and risked: "Where are you now?"

"The Piano, of course."

"Is Ralph Sampson there?"

Her answer was a hiccup of surprise. She was silent for a moment. At the other end of the line I could hear the murmur of people, the clatter of dishes. Probably a restaurant.

She recovered her voice: "Why ask me? I haven't seen him lately?"

"Where is he?"

"I don't know. Who is this talking? Mr. Troy?"

"Yes. I'll attend to Fay." I hung up.

The knob of the front door rattled slightly behind me. I froze with my hand on the telephone and watched the cut-glass knob as it slowly rotated, sparkling in the light from the living-room. The door swung open suddenly, and a man in a light topcoat stood in the opening. His silver head was hatless. He stepped inside like an actor coming on stage, shutting the door neatly with his left hand. His right hand was in the pocket of the topcoat. The pocket was pointed at me.

I faced him. "Who are you?"

"I know it isn't polite to answer one question with another." His voice was softened by a trace of south-of-England accent a long way from home. "But who are you?"

"If this is a stickup . . ."

The weight in his pocket nodded at me dumbly. He became more peremptory. "I asked you a simple question, old chap. Give me a simple answer."

"The name is Archer," I said. "Do you use bluing when you wash your hair? I had an aunt who said it was very effective."

His face didn't change. He showed his anger by speaking more precisely. "I dislike superfluous violence. Please don't make it necessary."

I could look down on the top of his head, see the scalp shining through the carefully parted hair. "You terrify me," I said. "An Italianate Englishman is a devil incarnate."

But the gun in his pocket was a small, intense refrigerating unit cooling off the hallway. His eyes had already turned to ice.

"And what do you do for a living, Mr. Archer?"

"I sell insurance. My hobby is stooging for gunmen." I reached for my wallet to show him my "insurance of all descriptions" card.

"No, keep your hands where I can see them. And guard your tongue, won't you?"

"Gladly. Don't expect me to sell you insurance. You're not a good risk, toting a gun in L. A."

The words went over his head and left it unruffled. "What are you doing here, Mr. Archer?"

"I brought Fay home."

"Are you a friend of hers?"

"Apparently. Are you?"

"I'll ask the questions. What do you plan to do next?"

"I was just going to call a taxi and go home."

"Perhaps you had better do that now," he said.

I picked up the receiver and called a Yellow Cab. He moved toward me lightly. His left hand palpated my chest and armpits, moved down my flanks and hips. I was glad I'd left my gun in the car, but I hated to be touched by him. His hands were epicene.

He stepped back and showed me his gun, a nickel-plated revolver, .32 or .38 caliber. I was calculating my chances of kicking him off balance and taking it.

His body stiffened slightly, and the gun came into focus like an eye. "No," he said. "I'm a quick shot, Mr. Archer. You'd stand no chance at all. Now turn around."

I turned. He jammed the gun into my back above the kidneys. "Into the bedroom."

He marched me into the lighted bedroom and turned me to face the door. I heard his quick feet cross the room, a drawer open and shut. The gun came back to my kidneys.

"What were you doing in here?"

"I wasn't in here. Fay turned on the light."

"Where is she now?"

"In the front room."

He walked me into the room where Mrs. Estabrook was lying, hidden by the back of the chesterfield. She had sunk into a stuporous sleep that resembled death. Her mouth was open, but she was no longer snoring. One of her arms hung down to the floor like an overfed white snake.

He looked at her with contempt, the contempt that silver might feel for sodden flesh.

"She never could hold her liquor."

"We were pub-crawling," I said. "We had a wizard do."

He looked at me sharply. "Evidently. Now why should you be interested in a bag of worms like this?"

"You're talking about the woman I love."

"My wife." A slight twitch of his nostrils proved that his face could move.

"Really?"

"I'm not a jealous man, Mr. Archer, but I must warn you to keep away from her. She has her own small circle of associates, and you simply wouldn't fit in. Fay's very tolerant, of course. I am less tolerant. Some of her associates aren't tolerant in the least."

"Are they all as wordy as you?"

He showed his small, regular teeth and subtly changed his posture. His torso leaned, and his head leaned sideways with it, glinting in the light. He was an obscene shape, a vicious boy alert and eager behind an old man's mask. The gun twirled on his finger like a silver wheel and came to rest pointed at my heart. "They have other ways of expressing themselves. Do I make myself clear?"

"The idea is a simple one to grasp." The sweat was cold on my back.

A car honked in the street. He went to the door and held it open for me. It was warmer outside.

chapter **10** *"I'm glad I called in,"* the driver said. "Saves me a dry run. I had a long haul out to Malibu. Four pigs called out to a beach party. They'll never get near the water."

The back of the cab still had a hothouse odor.

"You should of heard those women talk." He slowed for the stop sign at Sunset. "Going back to town?"

"Wait a minute." He stopped.

"Do you know of a place called the Piano?"

"The Wild Piano?" he said. "In West Hollywood. Sort of a bottle joint."

"Who runs it?"

"They never showed me their books," he said airily, shifting into gear. "You want to go there?"

"Why not?" I said. "The night is young." I was lying. The night was old and chilly, with a slow heartbeat. The tires whined like starved cats on the fog-sprinkled black-top. The neons along the Strip glared with insomnia.

The night was no longer young at the Wild Piano, but her heartbeat was artificially stimulated. It was on a badly lit sidestreet among a row of old duplexes shouldering each other across garbage-littered alleys. It had no sign, no plastic-and-plate-glass front. An arch of weather-browned stucco, peeling away like scabs, curved over the entrance. Above it a narrow balcony with a wrought iron railing masked heavily curtained windows.

A Negro doorman in uniform came out from under the arch and opened the door of the cab. I paid off the driver and followed him in. In the dim light from over the door I could see that the nap of his blue coat was worn down to the bare fiber. The brown leather door had been stained black around the handle by the pressure of many sweating hands. It opened into a deep, narrow room like a tunnel.

Another Negro in a waiter's jacket, a napkin over his arm, came to the door to meet me. His smile-stretched lips were indigo in the blue light that emanated from the walls. The walls were decorated with monochromatic blue nudes in various postures. There were white-clothed tables along them on either side, with an aisle between. A woman was playing a piano on a low platform at the far end of the room. She looked unreal through the smoke, a mechanical doll with clever hands and a rigid immovable back.

I handed my hat to a hat-check girl in a cubbyhole and asked for a table near the piano. The waiter skidded ahead of me down the aisle, his napkin fluttering like a pennon, trying to create the illusion that business was brisk. It wasn't. Two thirds of the tables were empty. The rest were occupied by couples. The men were a representative off-scouring of the better bars, putting off going home. Fat and thin, they were fish-faced in the blue aquarium light, fish-faced and oyster-eyed.

Most of their companions looked paid or willing to be paid. Two or three were blondes I had seen in chorus lines, with ingenue smiles fixed on their faces as if they could arrest the passage of time. Several were older women whose pneumatic bodies would keep them afloat for another year or two. These women were working hard with hands, with tongues, with eyes. If they slipped from the level of the Wild Piano, there were worse places to fall to.

A Mexican girl with a bored yellow face was sitting by herself at the table next to mine. Her eyes reached for me, turned away again.

"Scotch or bourbon, sir?" the waiter said.

"Bourbon and water. I'll mix it."

"Yes, sir. We have sandwiches."

I remembered that I was hungry. "Cheese."

"Very good, sir."

I looked at the piano, wondering if I was being too literal. The woman who called herself Betty had said she was at the piano. Its hoarse voice threaded the irregular laughter from the tables in melancholy counterpoint. The pianist's fingers moved in the keyboard mirror with a hurried fatality, as if the piano played itself and she had to keep up with it. Her tense bare shoulders were thin and shapely. Her hair poured down on them like tar and made them seem stark white. Her face was hidden.

"Hello, handsome. Buy me a drink."

The Mexican girl was standing by my chair. When I looked up she sat down. Her round-shouldered hipless body moved like a whip. Her low-cut gown was incongruous—clothes on a savage. She tried to smile, but her wooden face had never learned that art.

"I should buy you a pair of glasses."

She knew it was meant to be funny and that was all. "You are a funny boy. I like a funny boy." Her voice was guttural and forced, the voice you would expect from a wooden face.

"You wouldn't like me. But I'll buy you a drink."

She moved her eyes in order to express pleasure. They were solid and unchanging like lumps of resin. Her hands moved onto my arm and began to stroke it. "I like you, funny boy. Say something funny."

She didn't like me, and I didn't like her. She leaned forward to let me look down her dress. The breasts were little and tight, with pencil-sharp nipples. Her arms and upper lip were furred with black.

"On second thought I'll buy you hormones," I said.

"Is it something to eat? I am very hungry." She showed me her hungry white teeth by way of illustration.

"Why don't you take a bite of me?"

"You are kidding me," she said sulkily. But her hands continued working on my arm.

The waiter appeared and gave me a chance to break loose. He transferred from his tray to the table a small sandwich on a plate, a glass of water, a teacup with a half inch of whisky at the bottom, an empty teapot, and a glass of something he had telepathically brought along for the girl.

"That will be six dollars, sir."

"I beg your pardon."

"Two dollars per drink, sir. Two dollars for the sandwich."

I lifted the upper layer of the sandwich and looked at the slice of cheese it contained. It was as thin as gold leaf and almost as expensive. I put down a ten-dollar bill and left the change on the table. My primitive companion drank her fruit juice, glanced at the four ones, and went back to work on my arm.

"You have very passionate hands," I said; "only I happen to be waiting for Betty."

"Betty?" She flung a disdainful black glance at the pianist's back. "But Betty is arteest. She will not—" A gesture finished the sentence.

"Betty is the one for me."

Her lips came together with a red tip of tongue protruding as if she was going to spit. I signaled a waiter and ordered a drink for the woman at the piano. When I turned back to the Mexican girl she was gone.

The waiter pointed me out when he set down the drink on the piano, and the pianist turned to look. Her face was oval, so small and delicately modeled it looked pinched. Her eyes were indeterminate in color and meaning. She made no effort to smile. I raised my chin by way of invitation. Her head jerked negatively and bent over the keyboard again.

I watched her white hands picking their way through the

artificial boogie-woogie jungle. The music followed them like
giant footsteps rustling in metallic undergrowth. You could
see the shadow of the giant and hear his trip-hammer heartbeat. She was hot.

Then she changed her tune. Her left hand still drummed
and rolled in the bass, while her right hand elaborated a blues.
She began to sing in a hard, sibilant voice, frayed at the edges
but somehow moving:

> Brain's in my stomach,
> Heart's in my mouth,
> Want to go north—
> My feet point south.
> I got the psychosomatic blues.
> Doctor, doctor, doctor,
> Analyze my brain.
> Organize me, doctor.
> Doctor ease my pain—
> I got the psychosomatic blues.

She phrased her song with decadent intelligence. I didn't
like it, but it deserved a better audience than the chattering
room behind me. I clapped when it ended and ordered her
another drink.

She brought it to my table and sat down. She had a Tanagra
figurine body, small and perfect, poised timelessly somewhere
between twenty and thirty. "You like my music," she stated.
She inclined her forehead and looked up at me from under
it, the mannerism of a woman proud of her eyes. Their
brown-flecked irises were centerless and disturbing.

"You should be on Fifty-second Street."

"Don't think I wasn't. But you haven't been there for a
while, have you? The street has gone to the dogs."

"There's no percentage in this place. It's going to fold. Anybody can see the signs. Who runs it?"

"A man I know. Got a cigarette?"

When I lit it for her, she inhaled deeply. Her face unconsciously waited for the lift and drooped a little when it didn't come. She was a baby with an ageless face, sucking a dry bottle. The rims of her nostrils were bloodless, as white as snow, and that was no Freudian error.

"My name is Lew," I said. "I must have heard of you."

"I'm Betty Fraley." The statement had a margin of regret like a thin black border on a card. The name didn't mean anything to me, but it did to her.

"I remember you." I lied more boldly: "You got a tough break, Betty." All snowbirds wore stigmata of bad luck.

"You can say it twice. Two years in a white cell, and no piano. The conspiracy rap was a hummer. All they could prove was I needed it myself. They took me for my own good, they said. Their own good! They wanted publicity, and my name was known. It isn't any more, and if I ever kick the habit, it won't be with the help of the feds." Her red mouth twisted over the wet red end of the cigarette. "Two years without a piano."

"You do nicely for a girl that's out of practice."

"You think so? You should have heard me in Chicago when I was at my peak. I draped the piano over the beams in the ceiling and swung from the keys. You heard my records, maybe."

"Who hasn't?"

"Were they like I said?"

"Marvelous! I'm crazy about them."

But hot piano wasn't my dish, and I'd picked the wrong words or overdone my praise.

The bitterness of her mouth spread to her eyes and voice. "I don't believe you. Name one."

"It's been a long time."

"Did you like my *Gin Mill Blues?*"

"I did," I said with relief. "You do it better than Sullivan."

"You're a liar, Lew. I never recorded that number. Why would you want to make me talk too much?"

"I like your music."

"Yeah. You're probably tone-deaf." She looked intently into my face. The mutable eyes had hard, bright diamond centers. "You could be a cop, you know. You're not the type, but there's something about the way you look at things, wanting them but not liking them. You got cop's eyes—they want to see people hurt."

"Take it easy, Betty. You're only half psychic. I don't like to see people hurt, but I'm a cop."

"Narcotics?" Her face was brushed by white terror.

"Nothing like that. A private cop. I don't want anything from you. I just happen to like your music."

"You lie." In spite of her hatred and fear she was still whispering. Her voice was a dry rustle. "You're the one that answered Fay's phone and said you were Troy. What do you think you're after?"

"A man called Sampson. Don't tell me you haven't heard of him. You have."

"I never heard of him."

"That's not what you said on the phone."

"All right, I've seen him in here like anybody else. Does

that make me his nurse? Why come to me? He's just another flybar in my book."

"You came to me. Remember?"

She leaned toward me, projecting hatred like a magnetic field. "Get out of here and stay out."

"I'm staying."

"You think." She jerked a taut white hand at the waiter, who came running. "Call Puddler. This jerk's a private cop."

He looked at me with uncertainty tugging at his blue-black face.

"Take it easy," I said.

She stood up and went to the door behind the piano. "Puddler!" Every head in the room jerked up.

The door sprang open, and the man in the scarlet shirt came out. His small eyes moved from side to side, looking for trouble.

She pointed a finger at me. "Take him out and work him over. He's a peeper, trying to pump me."

I had time to run, but I lacked the inclination. Three runouts were too many in one day. I went to meet him and took the sucker punch. The scarred head rolled away easily. I tried with my right. He caught it on the forearm and moved in.

His dull eyes shifted. I had the funny feeling that they didn't recognize me. One fist came into my stomach. I dropped my guard. The other came into my neck below the ear.

My legs were caught by the edge of the platform. I fell against the piano. Consciousness went out in jangling discord, swallowed by the giant shadow.

chapter **11**   At the bottom of a black box a futile little man was sitting with his back against something
hard. Something equally hard was hitting him in the face.
First on one side of the jaw, then on the other. Every time
this happened his head bounced once against the hard surface
behind him. This distressing sequence—the blow followed
by the bounce—continued with monotonous regularity for
a considerable period of time. Each time the fist approached
his jaw the futile man snapped at it futilely with his aching
teeth. His arms, however, hung peacefully at his sides. His
legs were remarkably inert and distant.

A tall shadow appeared at the mouth of the alley, stood
one-legged like a stork for an instant, then limped grotesquely
toward us. Puddler was too absorbed in his work to notice.
The shadow straightened up behind him and swung one arm
high in the air. The arm came down with a dark object
swinging at the end of it. It made a cheerful sound, like
cracking walnuts, on the back of Puddler's head. He knelt in
front of me. I couldn't read his soul in his eyes because only
the whites were showing. I pushed him over backward.

Alan Taggert put his shoe on and squatted beside me. "We
better get out of here. I didn't hit him very hard."

"Let me know when you're going to hit him hard. I want
to be present."

My lips felt puffed. My legs were like remote and rebellious
colonies of my body. I established mandates over them and
got to my feet. It was just as well I couldn't stand on one
of them. I would have kicked the man on the pavement and
regretted it later—several years later.

Taggert took hold of my arm and pulled me toward the mouth of the alley. A taxi with one door open was standing at the curb. Across the street the stucco entrance of the Wild Piano was deserted. He pushed me into the cab and got in after me.

"Where do you want to go?"

My brain was a vacuum for an instant. Then anger surged into the vacuum. "Home to bed, but I'm not going. Swift's on Hollywood Boulevard."

"They're closed," the driver said.

"My car's in their parking lot." And my gun was in the car.

We were halfway there before my brain caught up with my tongue. "Where in hell did you come from?" I said to Taggert.

"Out of the everywhere into the here."

I snarled at him: "Don't double-talk. I'm not in the mood."

"Sorry," he said seriously. "I was looking for Sampson. There's a place back there called the Wild Piano. Sampson took me there once, and I thought I'd ask them about him."

"That's what I thought I'd do. You saw the answer they gave me."

"How did you happen to go there?"

I couldn't be bothered explaining. "I stumbled in. Then I stumbled out."

"I saw you coming out," he said.

"Did I walk out?"

"More or less. You had some help. I waited in the taxi to see what gave. When the bruiser took you into the alley I came in after you."

"I haven't thanked you," I said.

"Don't bother." He leaned toward me and said in an earnest whisper: "You really think Sampson's been kidnapped?"

"I'm not thinking so well just now. It's one idea I had when I was having ideas."

"Who would have kidnapped him?"

"There's a woman named Estabrook," I said, "a man named Troy. Ever meet him?"

"No, but I've heard of the Estabrook woman. She was with Sampson in Nevada a couple of months ago."

"In what capacity?" My bruised face felt like leering. I let it leer.

"I wouldn't know for sure. She went there by car. The plane was out of commission, and I was in Los Angeles with it. I never got to see her, but Sampson mentioned her to me. As far as I could tell, they sat around in the sun talking about religion. I think she's a sidekick of this holy man Claude. The one Sampson gave the mountain to."

"You should have told me before. That was her picture I showed you."

"I didn't know that."

"It doesn't matter now. I spent the evening with her. She was the woman I was with in the Valerio."

"She was?" He seemed astonished. "Does she know where Sampson is?"

"It's possible she does, but she wasn't saying. I'm going to pay her another visit now. And I could use some help. Her household is a rather violent one."

"Good!" said Taggert.

My reactions were still too slow, and I let him drive. He

tended to bank on the turns, but all went well until we got to the Estabrook house. It was dark. The Buick was gone from the driveway, and the garage was empty. I knocked on the front door with the muzzle of my gun. No answer.

"She must have gotten suspicious," Taggert said.

"We'll break in."

But the door was bolted and too strong for our shoulders. We went around to the back. In the yard I stumbled over a smooth, round object that turned out to be a beer bottle.

"Steady there, old man," Taggert said in a Rover Boy way. He seemed to be enjoying himself.

He flung himself with youthful abandon against the kitchen door. When we pushed together it splintered at the lock and gave. We went through the kitchen into the dark hall.

"You're not carrying a gun?" I said.

"No."

"But you know how to use one."

"Naturally. I prefer a machine gun," he bragged.

I handed him my automatic. "Make do with this." I went to the front door, pulled back the bolt, and opened it a crack. "If anybody comes let me know. Don't show yourself."

He took up his position with great solemnity, like a new sentry at Buckingham Palace. I went the rounds of the living-room, the dining-room, the kitchen, the bathroom, turning lights on and off. Those rooms were as I had seen them last. The bedroom was slightly different.

The difference was that the second drawer had nothing but stockings in it. And a used envelope, torn and empty, which was crumpled in a corner behind the stockings. The envelope was addressed to Mrs. Estabrook at the address I was visiting.

Someone had scrawled some words and figures in pencil on the back: "Avge. gross $2000. Avge. expense (Max) $500. Avge. net $1500. May—1500 × 31—46,500 less 6,500 (emerg.) —40,000. $\dfrac{40,000}{2} = 20,000$." It looked like a crude prospectus for a remarkably profitable business. One thing I knew for sure: the Wild Piano wasn't making that kind of money.

I turned the envelope over again. It was dated April 30, a week before, and postmarked Santa Maria. While that was sinking in, I heard a heavy motor growling in the road. I snapped off the light and moved into the hall.

A wave of light washed over the front of the house, poured in at the crack of the door where Taggert was standing. "Archer!" he whispered hoarsely.

Then he did a bold and foolish thing. He stepped out onto the porch, in the full white glare, and fired the gun in his hand.

"Hold it," I said, too late. The bullet rapped metal and whined away in richochet. There was no answering shot.

I elbowed past him and plunged down the front steps. A truck with a closed van was backing out of the drive in a hurry. I sprinted across the lawn and caught the truck in the road before it could pick up speed. The window was open on the right side of the cab. I hooked my arm through it and braced one foot on the fender. A thin white cadaver's face turned toward me over the wheel, its small frightened eyes gleaming. The truck stopped as if it had struck a stone wall. I lost my grip and fell in the road.

The truck backed away, changed gears with a grinding clash, and came toward me while I was still on my knees. The bright lights hypnotized me for a second. The roaring wheels bore down on me. I saw their intention and flung myself sideways, rolled to the curb. The truck passed ponderously over the place in the road where I had been, and went on up the street, the roar of its motor mounting in pitch and volume. Its license plate, if it had one, wasn't lighted. The back doors were windowless.

When I reached my car Taggert had started the engine. I pushed him out of the driver's seat and followed the truck. It was out of sight when we reached Sunset. There was no way of knowing whether it had turned toward the mountains or toward the sea.

I turned to Taggert, who was sitting rather forlornly with the gun in his lap. "Hold your fire when I tell you to."

"It was too late when you told me. I aimed over the driver's head, anyway, to force him out of the cab."

"He tried to run me down. He wouldn't have got away if you could be trusted with firearms."

"I'm sorry," he said contritely. "I guess I was trigger happy." He handed me the gun, butt foremost.

"Forget it." I turned left toward the city. "Did you get a good look at the truck?"

"I think it was army surplus, the kind they used for carrying personnel. Painted black, wasn't it?"

"Blue. What about the driver?"

"I couldn't make him out very well. He was wearing a peaked cap, that's all I could see."

"You didn't see his front plate?"

"I don't think there was any."

"That's too bad," I said. "It's barely possible Sampson was in that truck. Or has been."

"Really? Do you think we should go to the police?"

"I think we should. But first I'll have to talk to Mrs. Sampson. Did you phone her?"

"I couldn't get her. She was out with sleeping pills when I called her back. She can't sleep without them."

"I'll see her in the morning, then."

"Are you going to fly up with us?"

"I'll drive up. There's something I want to do first."

"What's that?"

"A little private business," I said flatly.

He was silent after that. I didn't want to talk. It was getting on toward dawn. The murky red cloud over the city was turning pale at the edges. The late-night traffic of cabs and private cars had dwindled to almost nothing, and the early-morning trucks were beginning to roll. I watched for a blue army surplus truck with a closed van and didn't see one.

I dropped Taggert at the Valerio and went home. A quart of milk was waiting on my doorstep. I took it in for company. The electric clock in the kitchen said twenty after four. I found a box of frozen oysters in the freezing compartment of the refrigerator and made an oyster stew. My wife had never liked oysters. Now I could sit at my kitchen table at any hour of the day or night and eat oysters to my heart's content, building up my virility.

I undressed and got into bed without looking at the empty twin bed on the other side of the room. In a way it was a relief not to have to explain to anyone what I had been doing all day.

chapter **12**   It was ten in the morning before I
got downtown. Peter Colton was at the flat-topped desk in
his office. He had been my colonel in Intelligence. When I
opened the ground-glass door he glanced up sharply from a
pile of police reports, then lowered his eyes immediately to
show that I wasn't welcome. He was a senior investigator in
the D.A.'s office, a heavy middle-aged man with cropped fair
hair and a violent nose like the prow of a speedboat inverted.
His office was a plaster cubicle with a single steel-framed window. I made myself uncomfortable on a hard-backed chair
against the wall.

After a while he pointed his nose at me. "What happened
to that which, for want of a better term, I choose to call your
face?"

"I got into an argument."

"And you want me to arrest the neighborhood bully." His
smile dragged down the corners of his mouth. "You'll have to
fight your own battles, my little man, unless of course there's
something in it for me."

"A popsicle," I said sourly, "and three sticks of bubble
gum."

"You attempt to bribe the forces of the law with three
sticks of bubble gum? Don't you realize that this is the atomic
age, my friend? Three sticks of bubble gum contain enough
primal energy to blow us all to bits."

"Forget it. The argument was with a wild piano."

"And you think I have nothing better to do with my time
than to go about putting the arm on berserk pianos? Or put-

ting on a vaudeville act with a run-down divorce detective? All right, spill it. You want something for nothing again."

"I'm giving you something. It could grow up to be the biggest thing in your life."

"And of course you want something in return."

"A little something," I admitted.

"Let's see the color of your story. In twenty-five words."

"Your time isn't that valuable."

"Five," he said, leaning his nose on the ball of his thumb.

"My client's husband left Burbank Airport day before yesterday in a black limousine, ownership unknown. He hasn't been seen since."

"Twenty-five."

"Shut up. Yesterday she got a letter in his handwriting asking for a hundred grand in bills."

"There isn't that much money. Not in bills."

"There is. They have it. What does it suggest to you?"

He had taken a sheaf of mimeographed sheets from the upper left-hand drawer of his desk and was scanning them in quick succession. "Kidnapping?" he said absently.

"It smells like a snatch to me. Could be my nostrils are insensate. What does the hot sheet say?"

"No black limousines in the last seventy-two hours. People with limousines look after them. Day before yesterday, you say. What time?"

I gave him the details.

"Isn't your client a little slow on the uptake?"

"She has a passion for discretion."

"But not for her husband, I take it. It would help if you gave me her name."

"Wait a minute. I told you I want something. Two things.

One, this isn't for publication. My client doesn't know I'm here. Besides, I want the guy back alive. Not dead."

"It's too big to sit on, Lew." He was up and walking, back and forth like a caged bear between the window and the door.

"You'll be getting it through official channels. Then it's out of my hands. In the meantime you can be doing something."

"For you?"

"For yourself. Start checking the car-rental agencies. That's number two. Number three is the Wild Piano—"

"That's enough." He flapped his hands in front of his face. "I'll wait for the official report, if there is any."

"Did I ever give you a bum lead?"

"Plenty, but we won't go into that. You could be doing a little exaggerating, you know."

"Why should I be pitching curves?"

"It's a cheap and easy way to get your leg work done." His eyes were narrowed to intelligent blue slits. "There's an awful lot of car rentals in the county."

"I'd do it myself but I have to go out of town. These people live in Santa Teresa."

"And their name?"

"Can I trust you?"

"Some. Further than you can see me."

"Sampson," I said. "Ralph Sampson."

"I've heard of him. And I see what you mean about the hundred grand."

"The trouble is we can't be sure what happened to him. We've got to wait."

"That's what you said." He swung on his heel to the window and spoke with his back to the room. "You also said something about the Wild Piano."

"That was before you said I was looking for cheap leg work."

"Don't tell me you've got feelings I can hurt."

"You merely disappoint me," I said. "I bring you a setup involving a hundred grand in cash and five million in capital assets. So you haggle over a day of your precious time."

"I don't work for myself, Lew." He turned on me suddenly. "Is Dwight Troy in this?"

"Who," I said, "is Dwight Troy?"

"Poison in a small package. He runs the Wild Piano."

"I thought there were laws against places like that. And people like him. Excuse my ignorance."

"You know who he is, then?"

"If he's a white-haired Englishman, yes." Colton nodded his head. "I met him once. He waved a gun at me for some reason. I left. It wasn't my job to take his gun away."

Colton moved his thick shoulders uncomfortably. "We've been trying to get him for years. He's smooth and versatile. He goes just so far in a racket, until his protection wears thin, then he shifts to something else. He rode high in the early thirties, running liquor from Baja California until that petered out. Since then he's had his ups and downs. He had a gambling pitch in Nevada for a while, but the syndicate forced him out. His pickings have been slender lately, I hear, but we're still waiting to take him."

"While you're waiting," I said, with heavy irony, "you could close the Wild Piano."

"We close it every six months," he snapped. "You should have seen it before the last raid, when it was the Rhinestone.

They had a one-way window upstairs for voyeurs and mas-
ochists, a regular act of a woman whipping a man, and such
stuff. We put an end to that."

"Who ran it then?"

"A woman by the name of Estabrook. And what happened
to her? She wasn't even prosecuted." He snorted angrily. "I
can't do anything about conditions like that. I'm not a politician."

"Neither is Troy," I said. "Do you know where he lives?"

"No. I asked you a question about him, Lew."

"So you did. The answer is I don't know. But he and
Sampson have been moving in some of the same circles.
You'd be smart to put a man on the Wild Piano."

"If we can spare one." He moved toward me unexpectedly
and put a heavy hand on my shoulder. "If you meet Troy
again, don't try to take his gun. It's been tried."

"Not by me."

"No," he said. "The men that tried it are dead."

chapter **13**   It was a two-hour drive at sixty from
Los Angeles to Santa Teresa. The sun was past its zenith
when I reached the Sampson house, declining toward the sea
through scattered clouds that made moving shadows on the
terraces. Felix admitted me and led me through the house to
the living-room.

It was so big the heavy furniture seemed sparse. The wall
that faced the sea was a single sheet of glass, with spun-glass
curtains at each end like gathered lengths of light. Mrs. Samp-

son was a life-size doll propped in a padded chair beside the giant window. She was fully dressed, in lime-colored silk jersey. Her gold-shod feet rested on a footstool. Not a hair of her bleached head was out of place. The metal wheelchair was beside the door.

She was motionless and silent, making a deliberate tableau that verged on the ridiculous as the seconds passed. When the silence had twisted my arm for a quarter of a minute, "Very nice," I said. "You were trying to get in touch with me?"

"You've taken your time about coming." The voice of the still mahogany face was petulant.

"I can't apologize. I've been working hard on your case, and I relayed my advice to you. Have you taken it?"

"In part. Come closer, Mr. Archer, and sit down. I'm perfectly harmless, really." She indicated an armchair facing her own. I moved across the room to it.

"Which part?"

"All of me," she said, with the carnivore smile. "My sting has been removed. But of course you mean the advice. Bert Graves is attending to the money now."

"Has he seen the police?"

"Not yet. I want to discuss that with you. But first you'd better read the letter."

She picked up an envelope from the coffee table beside her and tossed it to me. I took out the empty envelope I'd found in Mrs. Estabrook's drawer and compared the two. They differed in size and quality and the handwriting of the address. The only similarity was in the Santa Maria postmark. Sampson's letter was addressed to Mrs. Sampson and had been collected at four thirty the previous afternoon.

"What time did you get it?"

"About nine o'clock last night. It's special delivery, as you can see. Read it."

The letter was a single sheet of plain white typewriter paper covered on one side with a blue-ink scrawl:

Dear Elaine:

I am involved in a deal which came up suddenly, and I need some cash in a hurry. There are a number of bonds in our joint safety deposit box at the Bank of America. Albert Graves can identify those that are negotiable and arrange to have them cashed. I want you to cash bonds for me to the value of one hundred thousand dollars. I want no bills larger than fifties and hundreds. Do not permit the bank to mark them or record the numbers, since the deal I mentioned is confidential and highly important. Keep the money in my safe at home until you hear from me again, as you shortly will, or until I send a messenger bearing a letter of identification from me.

You will have to take Bert Graves into your confidence, of course, but it is of the outmost importance that you should not tell anyone else about this business. If you do, I stand to lose a very large profit and might even find myself on the wrong side of the law. It must be kept completely secret from everyone. That is why I am asking you to obtain the money for me, instead of going directly to my bank. I will be finished with this business within the week, and will see you soon.

My best love, and don't worry.

Ralph Sampson.

"It's carefully done," I said, "but not convincing. The reason he gives for not going to the bank himself sounds pretty weak. What does Graves think of it?"

"He pointed that out, too. He thinks it's a put-up job. But, as he says, it's my decision."

"Are you absolutely certain this is your husband's writing?"

"There's no doubt about that. And did you notice the spelling of 'utmost'? It's one of his favorite words, and he always misspells it. He even pronounces it 'outmost.' Ralph isn't a cultivated man."

"The question is, is he a living one?"

Her level blue eyes turned to me with dislike. "Do you really think it's as serious as that, Mr. Archer?"

"He doesn't normally do business like this, does he?"

"I know nothing about his ways of doing business. Actually he retired from business when we were married. He bought and sold some ranches during the war, but he didn't confide the details of the transactions to me."

"Have any of his transactions been illegal?"

"I simply don't know. He's perfectly capable of it. It's one of the things that ties my hands."

"What are the others?"

"I don't trust him," she said thinly. "I have no way of knowing what he intends to do. With all that money he may be planning a trip around the world. Perhaps he intends to leave me. I don't know."

"I don't either, but this is my guess. Your husband is being held for ransom. He wrote this letter from dictation with a gun at his head. If it was really a business deal, he'd have no reason to write to you. Graves has his power of attorney. But kidnappers prefer to deal with the victim's wife. It makes things easier for them."

"What am I going to do?" she said, in a strained voice.

"Follow instructions to the letter, except that you should bring in the police. Not in an obvious or public way, but so they'll be standing by. You see, Mrs. Sampson, the easy way for kidnappers to dispose of a victim, after the money's been collected, is to blow his brains out and leave him. He's got to be found before that happens, and I can't do it alone."

"You seem very sure he's been kidnapped. Have you found out anything you haven't told me?"

"Quite a few things. They add up to the fact that your husband's been keeping bad company."

"I knew it." Her face slipped out of control for an instant, sprang into curves of triumph. "He loves to pose as a family man and a good father, but he's never fooled me."

"Very bad company," I said heavily. "As bad as there is in Los Angeles, and that's as bad as there is."

"He's always had a taste for low companions—" She broke off suddenly, raising her eyes to the door behind me.

Miranda was standing there. Wearing a gray gabardine suit that emphasized her height, her copper hair swept up on top of her head, she looked like an older sister of the girl I'd met the day before. But her eyes were wide with fury, and her words came out in a rush.

"You dare to say that about my father! He may be dying, and all you care about is proving something against him."

"Is that all I care about, dear?" The brown face was impassive again. Only the pale eyes moved, and the carefully painted mouth.

"Don't 'dear' me." Miranda strode toward us. Even in

anger her body had the grace of a young cat. She showed her claws. "All you really care about is yourself. If I ever saw a narcissist, you're one, Elaine. With your precious vanity, your primping, and your curling, and your special hairdresser, and your diet—it's all for your own benefit, isn't it?—so you can go on loving yourself. You surely don't expect anyone else to love you."

"Not you, certainly," the older woman said coolly. "The thought repels me. But what do you care about, my dear? Alan Taggert, perhaps? I believe you spent last night with him, Miranda."

"I didn't. You lie."

She was standing over her stepmother with her back to me. I was embarrassed, but I stayed where I was, balanced on the edge of my chair. I'd seen verbal cat fights end in violence more than once.

"Did Alan stand you up again? When is he going to marry you?"

"Never! I wouldn't have him." Miranda's voice was breaking. She was too young and vulnerable to stand the quarrel for long. "It's easy for you to make fun of me; you've never cared for anyone. You're frigid, that's what you are. My father wouldn't be God knows where if you'd given him any love. You made him come out here to California, away from all his friends, and now you've driven him away from his own house."

"Nonsense!" But Mrs. Sampson too was showing the strain. "I want you to think that over, Miranda. You've hated me from the beginning and sided against me whether I was right or wrong. Your brother was fairer to me—"

"You leave Bob out of this. I know you had him under

your thumb, but it's no credit to you. It pleased your vanity, didn't it, to have your stepson dancing attendance?"

"That's enough," Mrs. Sampson said hoarsely. "Go away, you wretched girl."

Miranda didn't move, but she fell silent. I turned in my seat and looked out the window. Below the terraced lawn a stone walk led out to a pergola that stood on the edge of the bluff overlooking the sea. It was a small octagonal building with a conical roof, completely walled with glass. Through it and beyond it I could see the shifting colors of the ocean: green and white where the surf began, sage-honey-colored in the kelp zone further out, then deep-water blue to the deep-sky-blue horizon.

My eye was caught by an unexpected movement beyond the belt of white water where the waves began to break. A little black disk skimmed out along the surface, skipped from wave to wave, and sank out of sight. Another followed it a moment later. The source of the skimming objects was too near shore to be seen, hidden by the steep fall of the cliff. When six or seven had skipped along the water and disappeared, there were no more. Unwillingly I turned to the silent room.

Miranda was still standing above the other woman's chair, but her posture had altered. Her body had come unstarched. One of her hands was lifted from her side toward her step-mother, not in anger. "I'm sorry, Elaine." I couldn't see her face.

Mrs. Sampson's was visible. It was hard and clever. "You hurt me," she said. "You can't expect me to forgive you."

"You hurt me too," with a sobbing rhythm. "You mustn't throw Alan in my face."

"Then don't throw yourself at his head. No, I don't really mean that, and you know it. I think you ought to marry him. You want to, don't you?"

"Yes. But you know how father feels about it. Not to mention Alan."

"You take care of Alan," Mrs. Sampson said, almost gaily, "and I'll take care of your father."

"Will you really?"

"I give you my word. Now please go away, Miranda. I'm dreadfully tired." She glanced at me. "All this must have been very instructive to Mr. Archer."

"I beg your pardon?" I said. "I was admiring your private view."

"Yes, lovely, isn't it?" She called to Miranda, who had started out of the room: "Stay if you wish, dear. I'm going upstairs."

She lifted a silver handbell that stood on the table beside her. Its sudden peal was like the bell at the end of a round. Miranda completed the picture by sitting down, with her face averted, in a far corner of the room.

"You've seen us at our worst," Mrs. Sampson said to me. "Please don't judge us by it. I've decided to do as you say."

"Shall I call the police?"

"Bert Graves will do it. He's familiar with all the Santa Teresa authorities. He should be here any minute."

Mrs. Kromberg, the housekeeper, entered the room and wheeled the rubber-tired chair across the carpet. Almost effortlessly she raised Mrs. Sampson in her arms and placed her in the chair. They left the room in silence.

An electric motor murmured somewhere in the house as Mrs. Sampson ascended toward heaven.

***chapter* 14** I sat down beside Miranda on the divan in the corner of the room. She refused to look at me.

"You must think we're terrible people," she said. "To fight like that in public."

"You seem to have something to fight about."

"I don't really know. Elaine can be so sweet at times, but she's always hated me, I think. Bob was her pet. He was my brother, you know."

"Killed in the war?"

"Yes. He was everything I'm not. Strong and controlled and good at everything he tried. They gave him the Navy Cross posthumously. Elaine worshipped the ground he walked on. I used to wonder if she was in love with him. But of course we all loved him. Our family's been quite different since he died and since we came out here. Father's gone to pieces, and Elaine's come up with this fake paralysis, and I'm all mixed up. But I'm talking much too much, aren't I?" The turning of her half-averted head to me was a lovely gesture. Her mouth was soft and tremulous, her large eyes were blind with thought.

"I don't mind."

"Thank you." She smiled. "I have no one to talk to, you see. I used to think I was lucky, with all of father's money behind me. I was an arrogant little bitch—maybe I still am. But I've learned that money can cut you off from people. We haven't got what it takes for the Santa Teresa social life, the international-Hollywood set, and we have no friends here. I suppose I shouldn't blame Elaine for that, but she was the one that insisted we come here to live during the war. My mistake was leaving school."

"Where did you go?"

"Radcliffe. I didn't fit in too well, but I had friends in Boston. They fired me for insubordination last year. I should have gone back. They would have taken me, but I was too proud to apologize. Too arrogant. I thought I could live with father, and he tried to be good to me, but it didn't work out. He hasn't got along with Elaine for years. There's always tension in the house. And now something's happened to him."

"We'll get him back," I said. But I felt that I should hedge. "Anyway, you have other friends. Alan and Bert, for example."

"Alan doesn't really care for me. I thought he did once— no, I don't want to talk about him. And Bert Graves isn't my friend. He wants to marry me, and that's quite different. You can't relax with a man that wants to marry you."

"He loves you, by all the signs."

"I know he does." She raised her round, proud chin. "That's why I can't relax with him. And why he bores me."

"You're asking for a hell of a lot, Miranda." And I was talking a hell of a lot, talking like somebody out of *Miles Standish*. "Things never work out quite perfectly no matter how hard you push them. You're romantic, and an egotist. Some day you'll come down to earth so hard you'll probably break your neck. Or fracture your ego, anyway, I hope."

"I told you I was an arrogant bitch," she said, too lightly and easily. "Is there any charge for the diagnosis?"

"Don't go arrogant on me now. You already have once."

She opened her eyes very wide in demure parody. "Kissing you yesterday?"

"I won't pretend I didn't like it. I did. But it made me mad. I resent being used for other people's purposes."

"And what were my sinister purposes?"

"Not sinister. Sophomore stuff. You should be able to think of better ways to fascinate Taggert."

"Leave him out of this." Her tone was sharp, but then she softened it. "Did it make you very mad?"

"This mad."

I took hold of her shoulders with my hands, of her mouth with mine. Her mouth was half open and hot. Her body was cool and firm from breast to knee. She didn't struggle. Neither did she respond.

"Did you get any satisfaction out of that?" she said, when I released her.

I looked into her wide green eyes. They were candid and steady, but they had murky depths. I wondered what went on in those sea depths, and how long it had been going on.

"It salved my ego."

She laughed. "It salved your lips, at least. There's lipstick on them."

I wiped my mouth with my handkerchief. "How old are you?"

"Twenty. Old enough for your sinister purposes. Do you think I act like a child?"

"You're a woman." I looked at her body deliberately— round breasts, straight flanks, round hips, straight round legs —until she squirmed. "That involves certain responsibilities."

"I know." Her voice was harsh with self-reproach. "I shouldn't fling myself around. You've seen a lot of life, haven't you?"

It was a girlish question, but I answered her seriously. "Too much, of one kind. I make my living seeing a lot of life."

"I guess I haven't seen enough. I'm sorry for making you mad." She leaned toward me suddenly and kissed my cheek very lightly.

I felt a letdown, because it was the kind of kiss a niece might give to an uncle. Well, I had fifteen years on her. The letdown didn't last. Bert Graves had twenty.

There was the sound of a car in the drive, then movement in the house.

"That must be Bert now," she said.

We were standing well apart when he entered the room. But he gave me a single glance, veiled and questioning and hurt, before he found control of his face. Even then there were vertical lines of anxiety between his eyebrows. He looked as if he hadn't slept. But he moved with speed and decision, cat-footed for a heavy man. His body, at least, was glad to get into action. He said hello to Miranda and turned to me.

"What do you say, Lew?"

"Did you get the money?"

He took the calfskin brief case from under his arm, unlocked it with a key, and dumped its contents on the coffee table—a dozen or more oblong packages wrapped in brown bank paper and tied together with red tape.

"One hundred thousand dollars," he said. "A thousand fifties and five hundred hundreds. God knows what we're going to do with it."

"Put it in the safe for now. There's one in the house, isn't there?"

"Yes," Miranda said. "In father's study. The combination's in his desk."

"And another thing. You need protection for this money and the people in this house."

Graves turned to me with the brown packages in his hand. "What about you?"

"I'm not going to be here. Get one of the sheriff's deputies to come out. It's what they're for."

"Mrs. Sampson wouldn't let me call them."

"She will now. She wants you to turn the whole thing over to the police."

"Good! She's getting some sense. I'll put this stuff away and get on the phone."

"See them in person, Bert."

"Why?"

"Because," I said, "this has some of the earmarks of an inside job. Somebody in this house could be interested in the conversation."

"You're ahead of me, but I see what you mean. The letter shows inside knowledge, which they might or might not have got from Sampson. Assuming there is a 'they,' and he has been kidnapped."

"We'll work on that assumption till another turns up. And for God's sake make the cops go easy. We can't afford to frighten them. Not if we want Sampson alive."

"I understand that. But where are you going to be?"

"This envelope is postmarked Santa Maria." I didn't bother telling him about the other envelope in my pocket. "There's a chance he may be there on legitimate business. Or illegitimate business, for that matter. I'm going there."

"I've never heard of his doing any business there. Still, it might be worth looking into."

"Have you tried the ranch?" Miranda said to Graves.

"I called the superintendent this morning. They haven't heard from him."

"What ranch is that?" I said.

"Father has a ranch on the other side of Bakersfield. A vegetable ranch. He wouldn't be likely to go there now, though, on account of the trouble."

"The field workers are out on strike," Graves said. "They've been out for a couple of months, and there's been some violence. It's a nasty situation."

"Could it have anything to do with this one?"

"I doubt it."

"You know," Miranda said, "he may be at the Temple. When he was there before, his letters came through Santa Maria."

"The Temple?" Once or twice before, I'd caught myself slipping off the edge of the case into a fairy tale. It was one of the occupational hazards of working in California, but it irked me.

"The Temple in the Clouds, the place he gave to Claude. Father spent a couple of days there in the early spring. It's in the mountains near Santa Maria."

"And who," I said, "is Claude?"

"I told you about him," Graves said. "The holy man he gave the mountain to. He's made the lodge over into some kind of a temple."

"Claude's a phony," Miranda put in. "He wears his hair long and never cuts his beard and talks like a bad imitation of Walt Whitman."

"Have you been up there?" I asked her.

"I drove Ralph up, but I left when Claude started to talk.

I couldn't bear him. He's a dirty old goat with a foghorn voice and the nastiest eyes I ever looked into."

"How about taking me there now?"

"All right. I'll put on a sweater."

Graves' mouth moved silently as if he was going to protest. He watched her anxiously as she left the room.

"I'll bring her home safely," I said. I should have held my tongue.

He moved toward me with his head down like a bull's, a big man and still hard. His arms were stiff at his sides. The fists were clenched at the end of them.

"Listen to me, Archer," he said in a monotone. "Wipe the lipstick off your cheek or I'll wipe it off for you."

I tried to cover my embarrassment with a smile. "I'd take you, Bert. I've had a lot of practice handling jealous males."

"That may be. But keep your hands off Miranda, or I'll spoil your good looks."

I rubbed my left cheek where Miranda had left her mark. "Don't get her wrong—"

"I suppose it was Mrs. Sampson you were playing kissing games with?" He uttered a small heartbroken laugh. "No soap!"

"It was Miranda, and it wasn't a game. She was feeling low and I talked to her and she kissed me once. It didn't mean a thing. Purely a filial kiss."

"I'd like to believe you," he said uncertainly. "You know how I feel about Miranda."

"She told me."

"What did she say?"

"That you were in love with her."

"I'm glad she knows that, anyway. I wish she'd talk to me when she's feeling low." He smiled bitterly. "How do you do it, Lew?"

"Don't come to me with your heart problems. I'll foul you up for sure. I have one little piece of advice, though."

"Shoot."

"Take it easy," I said. "Just take it easy. We've got a big job on our hands and we've got to pull together. I'm no threat to your love life and I wouldn't be if I could. And while I'm being blunt, I don't think Taggert is, either. He simply isn't interested."

"Thanks," he said in a harsh, forced voice. He wasn't the kind of man who went in for intimate confessions. But he added miserably: "She's so much younger than I am. Taggert has youth and looks."

There was a soft plopping of feet in the hall outside the door, and Taggert appeared in the doorway as if on cue. "Did somebody take my name in vain?"

He was naked except for wet bathing trunks, wide-shouldered, narrow-waisted and long-legged. With the wet dark hair curling on his small skull, the lazy smile on his face, he could have posed for the Greeks as a youthful god. Bert Graves looked him over with dislike and said slowly:

"I was just telling Archer how handsome I thought you were."

The smile contracted slightly but stayed on his face. "That sounds like a left-handed compliment, but what the hell! Hello, Archer, anything new?"

"No," I said. "And I was telling Graves that you're not interested in Miranda."

"Right you are," he answered airily. "She's a nice girl but

not for me. Now if you'll excuse me I'll put on some clothes."

"Gladly," Graves said.

But I called him back: "Wait a minute. Do you have a gun?"

"A pair of target pistols. .32's."

"Load one and keep it on you, eh? Stick around the house and keep your eyes open. Try not to be trigger-happy."

"I learned my lesson," he said cheerfully. "Do you expect something to break?"

"No, but if something does, you'll want to be ready. Will you do what I said?"

"I sure will."

"He's not a bad kid," Graves said, when he was gone, "but I can't stand the sight of him. It's funny; I've never been jealous before."

"Ever been in love before?"

"Not until now." He stood with his shoulders bowed, burdened by fatality and exaltation and despair. He was in love for the first time and for keeps. I was sorry for him.

"Tell me," he said, "what was Miranda feeling low about? This business of her father?"

"Partly that. She feels the family's been going to pieces. She needs some sort of steady backing."

"I know she does. It's one reason I want to marry her. There are other reasons, of course; I don't have to tell you that."

"No," I said. I risked a candid question. "Is money one of them?"

He glanced at me sharply. "Miranda has no money of her own."

"She will have, though?"

"She will have, naturally, when her father dies. I wrote his will for him, and she gets half. I don't object to the money—" he smiled wryly "—but I'm not a fortune-hunter, if that's what you mean."

"It isn't. She might come into that money sooner than you think, though. The old man's been running in some fast and funny circles in L. A. Did he ever mention a Mrs. Estabrook? Fay Estabrook? Or a man called Troy?"

"You know Troy? What sort of a character is he, anyway?"

"A gunman," I said. "I've heard that he's done murders."

"I'm not surprised. I tried to tell Sampson to keep away from Troy, but Sampson thinks he's fine."

"Have you met Troy?"

"Sampson introduced me to him in Las Vegas a couple of months ago. The three of us went the rounds, and a lot of people seemed to know him. All the croupiers knew him, if that's a recommendation."

"It isn't. But he had his own place in Las Vegas at one time. He's done a lot of things. And I don't think kidnapping would be beneath his dignity. How did Troy happen to be with Sampson?"

"I got the impression that he worked for Sampson, but I couldn't be sure. He's a queer fish. He watched me and Sampson gamble, but he wouldn't himself. I dropped an even thousand that night. Sampson won four thousand. To him that hath shall be given." He smiled ruefully.

"Maybe Troy was making a good impression," I said.

"Maybe. The bastard gave me the creeps. Do you think he's mixed up in this?"

"I'm trying to find out," I said. "Does Sampson need money, Bert?"

"Hell, no! He's a millionaire."

"Why would he go into business with a jerk like Troy?"

"The time hangs heavy on his hands. The royalties roll in from Texas and Oklahoma, and he gets bored. Sampson's a natural money-maker the way I'm a natural money-loser. He's not happy unless he's making it; I'm not happy unless I'm losing it." He broke off short when Miranda entered the room.

"Ready?" she said. "Don't worry about me, Bert."

She pressed his shoulder with her hand. Her light-brown coat fell open in front, and her small sweatered breasts, pointed like weapons, were half impatient promise, half gradual threat. She had let down her hair and brushed it behind her ears. Her bright face slanted toward him like a challenge.

He kissed her cheek lightly and tenderly. I still felt sorry for him. He was a strong, intelligent man, but he looked a little stuffy beside her in his blue pin-stripe business suit. A little weary and old to tame a filly like Miranda.

chapter **15**   The pass road climbed through sloping fields of dust-colored chaparral and raw red cutbacks. By holding the accelerator to the floor I kept our speed at fifty. The road narrowed and twisted more abruptly as we went up. I caught quick glimpses of boulder-strewn slopes, mile-wide canyons lined with mountain oak and spanned by telephone cables. Once through a gap in the hills I saw the sea like a low blue cloud slanting away behind. Then the road looped round into landlocked mountain wilderness, grayed and chilled suddenly by the clouds in the pass.

The clouds looked heavy and dense from the outside. When we entered them they seemed to thin out, blowing across the road in whitish filaments. Barren and dim through the clouds, the mountainside shouldered us. In a 1946 car, with a late-model girl beside me, I could still imagine we were crossing the watershed between Colton's atomic age and the age of stone when men stood up on their hind legs and began to count time by the sun.

The fog grew denser, limiting my vision to twenty-five or thirty feet. I took the last hairpin curves in second. Then the road straightened out. At a definite point the laboring motor accelerated of its own accord, and we came out of the cloud. From the summit of the pass we could see the valley filled with sunlight like a bowl brimming with yellow butter, and the mountains clear and sharp on the other side.

"Isn't it glorious?" Miranda said. "No matter how cloudy it is on the Santa Teresa side, it's nearly always sunny in the valley. In the rainy season I often drive over by myself just to feel the sun."

"I like the sun."

"Do you really? I didn't think you'd go in for simple things like sun. You're the neon type, aren't you?"

"If you say so."

She was silent for a while, watching the leaping road, the blue sky streaming backward. The road cut straight and flat through the green-and-yellow checkerboard valley. With no one in sight but the Mexican braceros in the fields, I floor-boarded. The speedometer needle stuck halfway between eighty-five and ninety.

"What are you running away from, Archer?" she said, in a mocking tone.

"Not a thing. Do you want a serious answer?"

"It would be nice for a change."

"I like a little danger. Tame danger, controlled by me. It gives me a sense of power, I guess, to take my life in my hands and know damn well I'm not going to lose it."

"Unless we have a blowout."

"I've never had one."

"Tell me," she said, "is that why you do your kind of work? Because you like danger?"

"It's as good a reason as any. It wouldn't be true, though."

"Why, then?"

"I inherited the job from another man."

"Your father?"

"Myself when I was younger. I used to think the world was divided into good people and bad people, that you could pin responsibility for evil on certain definite people and punish the guilty. I'm still going through the motions. And talking too much."

"Don't stop."

"I'm fouled up. Why should I foul you up?"

"I am already. And I don't understand what you said."

"I'll take it from the beginning. When I went into police work in 1935, I believed that evil was a quality some people were born with, like a harelip. A cop's job was to find those people and put them away. But evil isn't so simple. Everybody has it in him, and whether it comes out in his actions depends on a number of things. Environment, opportunity, economic pressure, a piece of bad luck, a wrong friend. The trouble is a cop has to go on judging people by rule of thumb, and acting on the judgment."

"Do you judge people?"

"Everybody I meet. The graduates of the police schools make a big thing of scientific detection, and that has its place. But most of my work is watching people, and judging them."

"And you find evil in everybody?"

"Just about. Either I'm getting sharper or people are getting worse. And that could be. War and inflation always raise a crop of stinkers, and a lot of them have settled in California."

"You wouldn't be talking about our family?" she said.

"Not especially."

"Anyway, you can't blame Ralph on the war—not entirely. He's always been a bit of a stinker, at least since I've known him."

"All your life?"

"All my life."

"I didn't know you felt that way about him."

"I've tried to understand him," she said. "Maybe he had his points when he was young. He started out with nothing, you know. His father was a tenant farmer who never had land of his own. I can understand why Ralph spent his life acquiring land. But you'd think he'd be more sympathetic to poor people, because he was poor himself. The strikers on the ranch, for instance. Their living conditions are awful and their wages aren't decent, but Ralph won't admit it. He's been doing everything he can to starve them out and break the strike. He can't seem to see that Mexican field-workers are people."

"It's a common enough illusion, and a useful one. It makes it easier to gouge people if you don't admit they're human— I'm developing into quite a moralist in early middle age."

"Are you judging me?" she asked me, after a pause.

"Provisionally. The evidence isn't in. I'd say you have nearly everything, and could develop into nearly anything."

"Why 'nearly'? What's my big deficiency?"

"A tail on your kite. You can't speed up time. You have to pick up its beat and let it support you."

"You're a strange man," she said softly. "I didn't know you'd be able to say things like that. And do you judge yourself?"

"Not when I can help it, but I did last night. I was feeding alcohol to an alcoholic, and I saw my face in the mirror."

"What was the verdict?"

"The judge suspended sentence, but he gave me a tongue-lashing."

"And that's why you drive so fast?"

"Maybe it is."

"I do it for a different reason. I still think your reason is a kind of running away. Death wish."

"No jargon, please. Do you drive fast?"

"I've done a hundred and five on this road in the Caddie."

The rules of the game we were playing weren't clear yet, but I felt outplayed. "And what's your reason?"

"I do it when I'm bored. I pretend to myself I'm going to meet something—something utterly new. Something naked and bright, a moving target in the road."

My obscure resentment came out as fatherly advice. "You'll meet something new if you do it often. A smashed head and oblivion."

"Damn you!" she cried. "You said you liked danger, but you're as stuffy as Bert Graves."

"I'm sorry if I frightened you."

"Frightened me?" Her short laugh was thin and cracked

like a sea bird's cry. "All you men still have the Victorian hangover. I suppose you think woman's place is in the home, too?"

"Not my home."

The road began to twist restlessly and rise toward the sky. I let the gradient brake the car. At fifty we had nothing to say to each other.

chapter **16**   At a height that made me conscious of my breathing we came to a high-backed road of new gravel, barred by a closed wooden gate. A metal mailbox on the gatepost bore the name "Claude" in stencilled white letters. I opened the gate, and Miranda drove the car through.

"It's another mile," she said. "Do you trust me?"

"No, but I want to look at the scenery. I've never been here before."

Apart from the road the country looked as if no one had ever been there. A valley dotted with boulders and mountain evergreen opened below us as we spiraled upward. Far down among the trees I caught the slight brown shudder of a deer's movement and disappearance. Another deer went after it in a rocking-horse leap. The air was so clear and still I wouldn't have been surprised to hear the rustle of their hoofs. But there was no sound above the whine of the motor. Nothing to hear, and nothing to look at but light-saturated air and the bare stone face of the mountain opposite.

The car crawled over the rim of a saucer-shaped depression in the top of the mountain. Below us in the center of the mesa the Temple in the Clouds stood, hidden from everyone but hawks and airmen. It was a square one-storied structure of white-painted stone and adobe, built around a central court. There were a few outbuildings inside the wire fence that formed a kind of stockade around it. From one of them a thin black smoke was trickling up the sky.

Then something moved on the flat roof of the main building, something that had been so still my eyes had taken it for granted. An old man was squatting there with his legs folded under him. He rose with majestic slowness, a huge leather-brown figure. With the uncut tangles of his gray hair and beard standing out from his head, he looked like the rayed sun in an old map. He stooped deliberately to pick up a piece of cloth, which he wound around his naked middle. He raised one arm as if to tell us to be patient, and descended into the inner court.

Its ironbound door creaked open. He emerged and waddled to the gate, which he unlocked. I saw his eyes for the first time. They were milky blue, bland and conscienceless like an animal's. In spite of his great sun-blacked shoulders and the heavy beard that fanned across his chest, he had a womanish air. His rich self-conscious voice was a subtle blend of baritone and contralto.

"Greetings, greetings, my friends. Any traveler who comes to my out-of-the-way doorstep is welcome to share my fare. Hospitality stands high among the virtues, close to the supreme virtue of health itself."

"Thanks. Do we drive in?"

"Please leave the automobile outside the fence, my friend. Even the outer circle should not be sullied by the trappings of a mechanical civilization."

"I thought you knew him," I said to Miranda, as we got out of the car.

"I don't think he can see very well."

When we came nearer, his blue-white eyes peered at her face. He leaned toward her, and his straggling gray hair swung forward, brushing his shoulders.

"Hello, Claude," she said crisply.

"Why, Miss Sampson! I was not looking for a visit from youth and beauty today. Such youth! Such beauty!"

He breathed through his lips, which were very heavy and red. I looked at his feet to check his age. Shod in rope-soled sandals with thongs between the toes, they were gnarled and swollen: sixty-year-old feet.

"Thank you," she said unpleasantly. "I came to see Ralph, if he's here."

"But he isn't, Miss Sampson. I am alone here. I have sent my disciples away for the present." He smiled vaguely without uncovering his teeth. "I am an old eagle communing with the mountains and the sun."

"An old vulture!" Miranda said audibly. "Has Ralph been here recently?"

"Not for several months. He has promised me, but he has not yet come. Your father has spiritual potentialities, but he is still caged and confined by the material life. It is hard to draw him up into the azure world. It is painful for him to open his nature to the sun." He said it with a chanting rhythm, an almost liturgical beat.

"Do you mind if I look around?" I said. "To make sure he isn't here."

"I tell you I am alone." He turned to Miranda. "Who is this young man?"

"Mr. Archer. He's helping me look for Ralph."

"I see. I'm afraid you must take my word that he is not here, Mr. Archer. I cannot permit you to enter the inner circle, since you have not submitted to the rite of purification."

"I think I'll have a look around anyway."

"But that is not possible." He placed his hand on my shoulder. It was soft and thick and brown, like a fried fish. "You must not enter the temple. It would anger Mithras."

His breath was sour-sweet and foul in my nostrils. I picked his hand off my shoulder. "Have you been purified?"

He raised his innocent eyes to the sun. "You must not jest of these matters. I was a lost and sinful man, blind-hearted and sinful, till I entered the azure world. The sword of the sun slew the black bull of the flesh, and I was purified."

"And I'm the wild bull of the pampas," I said to myself.

Miranda stepped between us. "All this is nonsense. We're going in to look. I wouldn't take your word for anything, Claude."

He bowed his shaggy head and smiled a close-mouthed smile of sour benevolence that made my stomach queasy. "As you will, Miss Sampson. The sacrilege will rest upon your heads. I hope and trust that the wrath of Mithras will not be heavy."

She brushed past him disdainfully. I followed her through the arched doorway into the inner court. The red sun over the mountains to the west remained impassive. Without a look or another word Claude mounted the stone staircase inside the door and disappeared onto the roof.

The stone-paved court was empty. Its walls were lined with closed wooden doors. I pressed the latch of the nearest. It opened into an oak-raftered room that contained a built-in bed covered with dirty blankets, a scarred iron trunk, unlabeled, a cheap cardboard wardrobe, and the sour-sweet smell of Claude.

"The odor of sanctity," Miranda said, at my shoulder.

"Did your father actually stay here with Claude?"

"I'm afraid so." She wrinkled her nose. "He takes this sunworshipping nonsense seriously. It's all tied up with astrology in his mind."

"And he actually gave this place to Claude?"

"I don't know if he deeded it to him. He handed it over for Claude to use as a temple. I suppose he'll take it back sometime, if he can. And if he ever gets over this religious lunacy of his."

"It's a queer sort of hunting-lodge," I said.

"It's not really a hunting-lodge. He built it as a kind of hideout."

"A hideout from what?"

"War. This dates from Ralph's last phase, the pre-religious one. He was convinced that another war was just around the corner. This was to be his sanctuary if we were invaded. But he got over the fear last year, just before they started work on the bomb shelter. The plans for the shelter were all ready, too. He took refuge in astrology instead."

"I didn't use the word 'lunacy,'" I said. "You did. Were you serious?"

"Not really." She smiled a little bleakly. "Ralph doesn't seem so crazy if you understand him. He felt guilty, I think, because he made money out of the last war. And then there was Bob's death. Guilt can cause all sorts of irrational fears."

"You read another book," I said. "This time it was a psychology textbook."

Her reaction was surprising. "You make me sick, Archer. Don't you get bored with yourself playing the dumb detective?"

"Sure I get bored. I need something naked and bright. A moving target in the road."

"You!" She bit her lip, flushed, and turned away.

We went from room to room, opening and closing the doors. Most of the rooms had beds in them and very little else. In the big living-room at the end there were five or six straw pallets on the floor. It was narrow-windowed and thick-walled like a fortress, and the air smelled like the tank of a county jail.

"The disciples live well, whoever they are. Did you see any when you were here before?"

"No. But I didn't come inside."

"Some people are suckers for a pitch like Claude's. They'll hand over everything they own and get nothing in return but a starvation diet and the prospect of a nervous breakdown. But I've never heard of a sun-worshippers' monastery before. I wonder where the suckers are today."

We finished our circuit of the court without seeing anyone. I looked up at the roof. Claude was sitting with his face to the sun, his naked back to us. The flesh hung down in heavy folds from his flanks and hips. His head was moving jerkily back and forth, as if he was arguing with someone, but no sound came from him. Like a bearded woman who knew two sexual worlds, the great eunuch back and head outlined by the sun were strange and ridiculous and dreadful.

Miranda touched my arm. "Speaking of lunacy—"

"He's putting on an act," I said, and half believed it. "At least he was telling the truth about your father. Unless he's in one of the other buildings."

We crossed the gravel yard to the adobe with the smoking chimney. I looked in through the open door. A girl with a shawl over her head was sitting on her heels in front of a glowing fireplace stirring a bubbling pot. It was a five-gallon pot, and it was full of what looked like beans.

"It looks as if the disciples are coming for supper."

Without moving her shoulders the girl turned her head to look at us. The whites of her eyes shone like porcelain in the clay-colored Indian face.

"Have you seen an old man?" I asked her in Spanish.

She shrugged one calico shoulder in the general direction of the temple.

"Not that old man. One who is beardless. Beardless, fat, and rich. His name is Señor Sampson."

She shrugged both shoulders and turned back to her steaming pot. Claude's sandals crunched in the gravel behind us.

"I am not wholly alone, as you can see. There is my hand-maiden, but she is little better than an animal. If you have done with us, perhaps you will permit me to return to my meditation. Sunset is approaching, and I must pay my respects to the departing god."

Beside the adobe there was a galvanized iron shed with a padlocked door. "Before you go, open the shed."

Sighing, he took some keys from the folds of his body cloth. The shed contained a pile of bags and cartons, most of which were empty. There were several sacks of beans, a case of condensed milk, some overalls and work boots in a few of the cartons.

Claude stood in the doorway watching me. "My disciples sometimes work in the valley by the day. Such work in the vegetable fields is a form of worship."

He moved back to let me out. I noticed the imprint of a tire in the clay at the edge of the gravel where his foot had been. It was a wide truck tire. I'd seen the herringbone pattern of the tread before.

"I thought you didn't let mechanical trappings come inside the fence?"

He peered at the ground and came up smiling. "Only when necessary. A truck delivered some provisions the other day."

"I hope and trust it was purified?"

"The driver has been purified, yes."

"Good. I suppose that you'll be doing some housecleaning now that we've contaminated the place."

"It is between you and the god." With a backward glance at the declining sun he returned to his perch on the roof.

On the way back to the state highway I memorized the route so that I could drive it blind at night if I had to.

chapter **17**   Before we crossed the valley the red sun had plunged behind the clouds over the coastal range. The shadowed fields were empty. We passed a dozen truckloads of field-workers returning to their bunkhouses on the ranches. Crammed like cattle in the rattling vans of the trucks, they stood in patient silence, men, women, and children waiting for food and sleep and the next day's sunrise.

I drove carefully, feeling a little depressed, stalled in the
twilight period when day has run down and night hasn't
picked up speed.

The clouds flowed in the pass like a torrent of milk and
preceded us down the other side of the mountain, blending
with the gradual night and the deepening cold. Once or twice
on a curve Miranda leaned against me, trembling. I didn't
ask her whether she was cold or afraid. I didn't want to force
her to make a choice.

The clouds had rolled down the mountain all the way to
U.S. 101. From far up the pass road I could see the headlights
on the highway blurred enormous by the fog. While I was
waiting at the stop sign for a break in the highway traffic,
a pair of bright lights came up fast from the direction of
Santa Teresa. They suddenly swung toward us like wild eyes.
The speeding car was going to try to turn into the pass road.
Its brakes screamed, its rubber skittered and snarled. It wasn't
going to get past me.

"Head down," I said to Miranda, and tightened my grip
on the wheel.

The other driver straightened out, roared into second gear
at forty-five or fifty, spun in front of my bumper, and passed
on my right in the seven-foot space between me and the stop
sign. I caught a flashing glimpse of the driver's face, a thin,
pale face jaundiced by my fog lights, under a peaked leather
cap. His car was a dark limousine.

I backed and turned and started after it. The black-top was
slick from the wet, and I was slow in getting under way. The
red rear light hightailing up the road was swallowed by the
fog. It was no use anyway. He could turn off on any one of
the county roads that paralleled the highway. And perhaps

the best thing I could do for Sampson was to let the limousine go. I stopped so fast that Miranda had to brace both hands on the dashboard. My reflexes were getting violent.

"What on earth's the matter? He didn't actually crash us, you know."

"I wish he had."

"He's reckless, but he drives very well."

"Yeah. He's a moving target I'd like to hit some time."

She looked at me curiously. Shadowed from below by the dashlights, her face was dark, with huge bright eyes. "You're looking grim, Archer. Have I made you angry again?"

"Not you," I said. "It's waiting for a break in this case. I prefer direct action."

"I see." She sounded disappointed. "Please take me home now. I'm cold and hungry."

I turned in the shallow ditch and drove back across the highway to Cabrillo Canyon. Beyond the plow of yellow light that the fog lamps pushed ahead of us the trees and hedges hung in the thick air, ash-gray emanations abandoned by the sun. The landscape matched the clouded pattern in my skull. My thoughts were blind and slow, groping for a lead to the place where Ralph Sampson was hidden.

The lead was waiting in the mailbox at the entrance to Sampson's drive, and it took no cunning to find it. Miranda noticed it first. "Stop the car."

When she opened the door, I saw the white envelope stuck in the slot of the mailbox. "Wait. Let me handle it."

My tone held her still with one foot on the ground, one hand reaching for the envelope. I took it by one corner and wrapped it in a clean handkerchief. "There may be finger-prints."

"How do you know it's from Father?"

"I don't. You drive up to the house."

I unwrapped the envelope in the kitchen. The fluorescent tube in the ceiling cast a white morgue glow on the white enameled table. There was no name or address on the envelope. I slit one end and drew out the folded sheet it contained with my fingernails.

My heart dropped when I saw the printed letters pasted to the sheet of paper. The letters had been cut out individually and arranged in words, in the classic tradition of kidnapping. These were the words:

Mr. Sampson is well in good hands put one hunderd thousan dollars in plain paper parsel ty with string put parsel on grass in middle of road at south end of highway division oposite Fryers Road one mile south of Santa Teresa limits do this at nine oclock tonite after you leave parsel drive away imediately you will be watched drive away north direction Santa Teresa do not attent pollice ambush if you value Sampsons life you will be watched he will come home tomorrow if no ambush no attent to chase no marked bills

too bad for Sampson if you dont
freind of the family

"You were right," Miranda said, in a half whisper.

I wanted to say something consoling. All I could think of was—too bad for Sampson.

"Go and see if Graves is around," I said. She went immediately.

I leaned over the sheet of paper without touching it, and examined the cut-out letters. They varied widely in size and type, and were printed on smooth paper, probably cut from the advertising pages of a big-circulation magazine. The spelling pointed at semi-literacy, but you couldn't always tell. Some pretty well-educated people were poor spellers. And it might have been faked.

I had memorized the letter when Graves came into the kitchen with Taggert and Miranda trailing behind. He came toward me on heavy piston-quick legs, with an iron gleam in his eyes.

I pointed to the table. "That was in the mailbox—"

"Miranda told me."

"It may have been dropped a few minutes ago by a car that passed me on the highway."

Graves leaned over the letter and read it aloud to himself. Taggert stayed by Miranda in the doorway, uncertain whether he was wanted but quite at ease. Though physically they could have been sibs, Miranda was his temperamental opposite. Ugly blue patches had blossomed under her eyes. Her wide lips drooped sullenly over her fine, prominent teeth. She leaned against the doorjamb in a jagged, disconsolate pose.

Graves raised his head. "This is it. I'll get the deputy."

"Here now?"

"Yes. In the study with the money. And I'll call the sheriff."

"Has he got a fingerprint man?"

"The D.A.'s is better."

"Call him too. They're probably too smart to leave fresh prints, but there may be latent ones. It's hard to do cut-outs with gloves on."

"Right. Now what was that about a car that passed you?"

"Keep it to yourself for now. I'll handle that end."

"I guess you know what you're doing."

"I know what I'm not doing. I'm not getting Sampson bumped if I can help it."

"That's what's worrying me," he said, and went through the door so fast that Taggert had to jump back out of his way.

I glanced at Miranda. She looked ready to drop. "Make her eat something, Taggert."

"If I can."

He crossed the kitchen to the refrigerator. Her eyes followed him. I hated her for an instant. She was like a dog, a bitch in the rutting season.

"I couldn't possibly eat," she said. "Do you think he's alive?"

"Yes. But I thought you barely liked him."

"This letter makes it so real. It wasn't real before."

"It's too damned real! Now go away. Go and lie down." She wandered out of the room.

The deputy sheriff came in. He was a heavy, dark man in his thirties, wearing brown store clothes that didn't quite fit his shoulders, a lopsided look of surprise that didn't quite fit his face. His right hand rested on the gun in his hip holster as if to remind him that he had authority.

He said with tentative belligerence: "What goes on out here?"

"Nothing much. Kidnapping and extortion."

"What's this?" He reached for the letter on the table. I had to take hold of his wrist to keep him from touching it.

His black eyes glared dully into my face. "Who do you think you are?"

"The name is Archer. Settle down, officer. You have an evidence case?"

"Yeah, in the car."

"Get it, eh? We'll hold this for the fingerprint men."

He went out and came back with a black metal box. I dropped the letter into it, and he locked it. It seemed to give him great satisfaction.

"Take good care of it," I said, as he left the room with the box under his arm. "Don't let it out of your hands."

Taggert was standing by the open refrigerator with a half-eaten turkey drumstick in his fingers. "What do we do now?" he asked me, between bites.

"You stick around. You may see a little excitement. Got your gun?"

"Sure thing!" He patted the pocket of his jacket. "How do you think it was done? You think they grabbed Sampson when he left the airport in Burbank."

"I wouldn't know. Where's a phone?"

"There's one in the butler's pantry. Right through here." He opened a door at the end of the kitchen and closed it after me.

It was a small room lined with cupboards, with a single window over the copper sink, a wall telephone by the door. I asked long distance for Los Angeles. Peter Colton would be off duty, but he might have left a message.

The operator gave me his office, and Colton answered the phone himself.

"Lew speaking. It's a snatch. We got the ransom note a few minutes ago. The letter from Sampson was a gimmick to loosen things up. You better talk to the D.A. It probably happened in your territory when Sampson left the Burbank airport day before yesterday."

"They're taking things slow for kidnappers."

"They can afford to. They've got the operation blueprinted. Did you get anything on the black limousine?"

"Too much. There were twelve of them rented that day, but most of them look legit. All but two came back to the agencies the same day. The other two were taken for a week, paid in advance."

"Descriptions?"

"Number one—a Mrs. Ruth Dickson, blond dame, around forty, living at the Beverly Hills Hotel. We checked there, and she's registered but she wasn't in. Number two was a guy on his way to San Francisco. He hasn't turned in the car at that end; but it's only two days, and he has it for a week. Name of Lawrence Becker, a little thin guy not too well dressed—"

"That may be our man. Did you get the number?"

"Wait a minute, I have it here—62 S 895. It's a 1940 Lincoln."

"Agency?"

"The Deluxe in Pasadena. I'll go out there myself."

"Get the best description you can, and spread the word."

"Natch! But why the sudden enthusiasm, Lew?"

"I saw a man on the highway here who could fit your description. He passed me in a long black car about the time the ransom note was dropped. And the same Joe or his brother tried to run me down with a blue truck in Pacific Palisades this morning. He wears a peaked leather cap."

"Why didn't you put the arm on him?"

"The same reason you're not going to. We don't know

where Sampson is, and if we throw our weight around, we'll never find out. Put out the word for tailing purposes only."

"You telling me my business?"

"Apparently."

"All right. Any more helpful hints?"

"Plant a man in the Wild Piano when it opens. Just in case—"

"I've already assigned him. Is that all?"

"Have your office contact the Santa Teresa D.A. I'm turning the ransom note over to them for fingerprinting. Good night and thanks."

"Uh-huh."

He hung up, and the operator broke the connection. I kept the receiver to my ear, listening to the dead line. In the middle of the conversation there had been a click and crackle on the wire. It could have been a momentary break in the connection, or it could have been a receiver being lifted on another extension.

A full minute passed before I heard the faint metallic rustle of a receiver's being replaced somewhere in the house.

chapter **18** Mrs. Kromberg was in the kitchen with the cook, a flustered white-haired woman with motherly hips. They both jumped when I opened the door of the pantry.

"I was using the phone," I said.

Mrs. Kromberg managed a crumpled smile. "I didn't hear you in there."

"How many phones are there in the house?"

"Four or five. Five. Two upstairs, three down."

I gave up the idea of checking the phones. Too many people had access to them. "Where is everybody?"

"Mr. Graves called the staff together in the front room. He wanted to know if anybody saw the car that left the note."

"Did anybody?"

"No. I heard a car a while back, but I didn't think anything about it. They're always coming down here and turning around in the drive. They don't know it's dead end." She moved closer to me and whispered confidentially: "What was in the note, Mr. Archer?"

"They want money," I said as I went out.

Three other servants passed me in the hallway, two young Mexicans in gardener's clothes, walking in single file with their heads down, and Felix bringing up the rear. I raised a hand to him, but he didn't respond. His eyes were opaque and glittering like lumps of coal.

Graves was squatting in front of the fireplace in the living-room turning a charred log with a pair of tongs.

"What's the matter with the servants?" I asked him.

He stood up with a grunt and glanced at the door. "They seem to know they're under suspicion."

"I wish they didn't."

"I didn't say anything to give them the idea. They got it by osmosis. I simply asked them if they'd seen the car. What I really wanted, of course, was a look at their faces before they could close them up."

"You think it's an inside job, Bert?"

"Obviously it's not entirely one. But whoever put together that letter is too well posted. How did he know, for example, that the money would be ready for a nine-o'clock deadline?" He glanced at his watch. "Seventy minutes from now."

"Sheer blind faith, maybe."

"Maybe."

"We won't argue. You're probably right that it's partly an inside job. Did anyone see the car?"

"Mrs. Kromberg heard it. The others played dumb, or are."

"And nobody gave himself away?"

"No. These Mexicans and Filipinos are hard to read." He was careful to add: "Not that I've any reason to suspect the gardeners, or Felix either."

"What about Sampson himself?"

He looked at me ironically. "Don't try to be brilliant, Lew. You never were too strong on intuition."

"It's merely a suggestion. If Sampson pays an eighty-percent income tax, he could make himself a quick eighty grand by staging this."

"I admit it could be done—"

"It has been."

"But in Sampson's case it's fantastic."

"Don't tell me he's honest."

He picked up the tongs and struck the burning log. The sparks flew up like a swarm of bright wasps. "Not by everybody's standards. But he hasn't got the kind of brain for that sort of a setup. It's too risky. Besides, he doesn't need the money. His oil properties are valued around five million, but they're worth more like twenty-five in terms of income. A hundred thousand dollars is small change to Sampson. This kidnapping is the real thing, Lew. You can't get around it."

"I'd like to," I said. "So many kidnappings end up in a murder of convenience."

"This one doesn't have to," he said, in a deep growling voice, "and, by God, it isn't going to! We'll pay them their money, and if they don't come through with Sampson we'll hunt them down."

"I'm with you." But it was easier said than done. "Who delivers the lettuce?"

"Why not you?"

"For one thing, they may know me. And I have something else to do. You do it, Bert. And you'd better take Taggert along."

"I don't like him."

"He's a sharp kid, and he's not afraid of a gun. If anything goes wrong, you may need help."

"Nothing is going to go wrong. But I'll take him if you say so."

"I say so."

Mrs. Kromberg appeared in the hall doorway, nervously pulling at the front of her smock. "Mr. Graves?"

"Well?"

"I wish you'd talk to Miranda, Mr. Graves. I tried to take her up something to eat, and she wouldn't unlock her door. She wouldn't even answer."

"She'll be all right. I'll talk to her later. Leave her alone for now."

"I don't like it when she acts this way. She's so emotional."

"Forget it. Ask Mr. Taggert to meet me in the study, will you? And ask him to bring his pistols—loaded."

"Yes, sir." She was on the point of tears, but she compressed her heavy lips and went away.

When Graves turned from the door, I saw that she had communicated some of her anxiety to him. One of his cheeks was twitching slightly. His eyes were looking at something beyond the room.

"She's probably feeling guilty," he said, half to himself.

"Guilty about what?"

"Nothing tangible. I suppose it's basically because she hasn't been able to take her brother's place. She's watched the old man going downhill, and she probably feels he wouldn't have gone down so far and so fast if she could have got closer to him."

"She isn't his wife," I said. "What's Mrs. Sampson's reaction? Have you seen her?"

"A few minutes ago. She's taking it very nicely. Reading a novel, in fact. How do you like that?"

"I don't. Maybe she's the one that should be feeling guilty."

"It wouldn't help Miranda if she did. Miranda's a funny girl. She's very sensitive, but I don't think she knows it. She's always sticking her neck out, living beyond her emotional resources."

"Are you going to marry her, Bert?"

"I will if I can." He smiled wryly. "I've asked her more than once. She hasn't said no."

"You could take good care of her. She's ripe for marriage."

He looked at me in silence for a moment. His lips continued to smile, but his eyes flashed a hands-off signal. "She said you had quite a talk on your drive this afternoon."

"I gave her some fatherly advice," I said. "About driving too fast."

"As long as you keep it on the paternal level." Abruptly he changed the subject. "What about this character Claude? Could he be in on the kidnapping?"

"He could be in on anything. I wouldn't trust him with a burnt-out match. But I didn't get anything definite. He claimed he hadn't seen Sampson for months."

Straw-yellow fog lamps brushed the side of the house, and a moment later a car door slammed. "That must be the sheriff," Graves said. "It took him a hell of a long time."

The sheriff came in with a great show of haste, like a sprinter breasting the tape. He was a big man in a business suit, carrying a wide-brimmed rancher's hat. Like his clothes, his face was hybrid, half cop and half politician. The sternness of his jaw was denied by the softness of his mouth, a loosely folded mouth that liked women and drink and words.

He thrust out his hand to Graves. "I would have been here sooner, but you asked me to pick up Humphreys."

The other man, who had followed him quietly into the room, was wearing a tuxedo. "I was at a party," he said. "How are you, Bert?"

Graves introduced me. The sheriff's name was Spanner. Humphreys was the District Attorney. He was tall and balding, with the lean face and haunted eyes of an intellectual sharpshooter. He and Graves didn't shake hands. They were too close for that. Humphreys had been Deputy Prosecutor when Graves was District Attorney. I stood back and let Graves do the talking. He told them what they needed to know and left out what they didn't need to know.

When he had finished, the sheriff said: "The letter orders you to drive away in a northern direction. That means he'll be making his getaway in the other direction, toward Los Angeles."

"That's what it means," Graves said.

"Now if we set up a road block down the highway a piece, we should be able to catch him."

"We can't do that," I said in words of one syllable. "If we do, we can kiss good-bye to Sampson."

"But if we catch the kidnapper, we can make him talk—"

"Hold it, Joe," Humphreys put in. "We've got to assume that there are more than one. If we knock off one of them, the other or others will knock off Sampson. It's as clear as the nose on your face."

"And it's in the letter," I said. "Have you seen the letter?"

"Andrews has it," Humphreys said. "He's my fingerprint man."

"If he finds anything, you should check with the F.B.I. files." I sensed that I was making myself unpopular, but I had no time to be tactful and I didn't trust small-time cops to know their business. I turned to the sheriff: "Are you in touch with the L. A. County authorities?"

"Not yet. I felt I should assess the situation first."

"All right, this is the situation. Even if we obey instructions to the letter, there's a better than fifty-fifty chance that Sampson won't come out alive. He must be able to identify at least one of the gang—the one that picked him up in Burbank. That's bad for him. You'll make it worse if you try to trip the money pickup. You'll have a kidnapper in the county jail, and Sampson lying somewhere with his throat cut. The best thing you can do is get on the wires. Let Graves handle the business at this end."

Spanner's face was mottled with anger, his mouth half open to speak.

Humphreys cut him off. "That makes sense, Joe. It's not good law enforcement, but we've got to compromise. The thing is to save Sampson's life. What say we get back to town now?"

He stood up. The sheriff followed him out.

"Can we trust Spanner not to make his own arrangements?"

"I think so," Graves said slowly. "Humphreys will keep an eye on him."

"Humphreys sounds like a good head."

"The best. I worked with him for seven-odd years, and I never caught him in a bad mistake. I got him the appointment when I resigned." There was some regret in his voice.

"You should have stuck with the work," I said. "You got a lot of satisfaction out of it."

"And damned little money! I stuck with it for ten years, and I ended up in debt." He gave me a sly look. "Why did you quit the Long Beach force, Lew?"

"The money wasn't the main thing. I couldn't stand podex osculation. And I didn't like dirty politics. Anyway, I didn't quit, I was fired."

"All right, you win." He glanced at his watch again. It was nearly eight thirty. "Time to get on our horse."

Alan Taggert was in the study, in a tan trench coat that bunched at the waist and made his shoulders look huge. He brought his hands out of his pockets with a gun in each fist. Graves took one, and Taggert kept the other. They were .32 target pistols with slender blue-steel snouts and prominent sights.

"Remember," I said, for Taggert's benefit, "no shooting unless you're shot at."

"Aren't you coming along?"

"No." I said to Graves: "You know the corner at Fryers Road?"

"Yes."

"There's no cover around?"

"Not a thing. The open beach on one side, and the cut-bank on the other."

"There wouldn't be. You go ahead in your car. I'll tag along behind and park a mile or so down the highway."

"You're not going to try a fast one?"

"Not me. I just want to see him go by. I'll meet you at the filling station at the city limits afterward. The Last Chance."

"Right." Graves twirled the knobs of the wall safe.

From the city limits to Fryers Road the highway was four-lane, a mile-long shelf cut into the bluffs that stood along the shore. It was divided in the middle by a strip of turf between concrete curbs. At the intersection with Fryers Road the turf ended and the highway narrowed to three lanes. Graves's Studebaker made a quick U turn at the intersection and parked with its lights burning on the shoulder of the highway.

It was a good place for the purpose, a bare corner rimmed on the right by a line of white posts. The entrance to Fryers Road was a gray-black hole in the side of the bluff. There wasn't a house in sight, or a tree. The cars on the highway were few and far between.

It was ten minutes to nine by my dashboard clock. I waved to Taggert and Graves and drove on past them. It was seven tenths of a mile to the next side road. I checked it on my mileage. Two hundred yards beyond this side road a parking space for sightseers had been built up over the beach on the

right side of the highway. I turned off and parked with the
lights out and the nose of the car pointed south. It was seven
minutes to nine. If everything went on schedule, the pay-off
car should pass me in ten minutes.

The fog closed around the car when it stopped, rising from
the shore like an impossible gray tide. A few pairs of headlights went north through the fog like the eyes of deep-sea
fish. Below the guardrail the sea breathed and gargled in the
darkness. At two minutes after nine the rushing headlights
came around the curve from the direction of Fryers Road.

The plunging car wheeled sharply before it reached me and
turned up the side road to the left. I couldn't see its color or
shape but I heard it losing rubber. The driver's technique
seemed familiar.

Leaving my lights out, I drove across the highway and
along its shoulder to the side road. Before I reached it I heard
three sounds, remote and muffled by the fog. The banshee
wail of brakes, the sound of a shot, the ascending roar of a
motor picking up speed.

The trough of the side road was filled with diffused white
light. I stopped my car a few feet short of the intersection.
Another car came out of the side road and turned left in
front of me toward Los Angeles. It was a long-nosed convertible painted light cream. I couldn't see the driver through
the blurred side window, but I thought I saw a dark mass of
woman's hair. I wasn't in position to give chase, and I couldn't
have anyway.

I switched on my fog lamps and turned up the road. A few
hundred yards from the highway a car was standing with two
of its wheels in the ditch. I parked behind it and got out with
the gun in my hand. It was a black limousine, a prewar Lin-

coln custom job. The engine was idling and the lights were on. The license number was 6 2 S 895. I opened the front door with my left hand, my gun cocked in my right.

A little man leaned toward me, peering into the fog with intent dead eyes. I caught him before he fell out. I'd been feeling death in my bones for twenty-four hours.

***chapter* 19** He was still wearing his leather cap sharply tilted on the left side of his head. There was a round hole in the cap above his left ear. The left side of his face was peppered with black powder burns. His head had been knocked askew by the force of the bullet, and rolled on his shoulder when I pushed him upright. His black-nailed hands slipped off the steering wheel and dangled at his sides.

Holding him up in the seat with one hand, I went through his pockets with the other. The side pockets of his leather windbreaker contained a windproof lighter smelling of gasoline, a cheap wooden case half full of cigarettes rolled in brown wheat-straw paper, and a four-inch spring-knife. There was a worn sharkskin wallet in the hip pocket of his levis, containing eighteen or twenty dollars in small bills and a California driver's license recently issued to one Lawrence Becker. The address on the license was a cheap Los Angeles hotel teetering on the edge of Skid Row. It wouldn't be his address, and Lawrence Becker wouldn't be his name.

The left side pocket of the levis held a dirty comb in a leatherette case. The other pocket held a heavy bunch of car keys on a chain—keys for every make of car from Chevrolet to Cadillac—and a half-used book of matches labeled: "Souvenir of The Corner, Cocktails and Steaks, Highway 101 South of Buenavista." He had nothing on under his windbreaker but a T-shirt.

There were a few short marijuana butts in the dashboard ash tray, but the rest of the car was as clean as a whistle. Not even a registration card in the glove compartment, nor a hundred thousand dollars in moderate-sized bills.

I put the things back in his pockets and propped him up in the seat, slamming the door to hold him. I looked back once before I got into my car. The lights of the Lincoln were still burning, the idling motor still sending out a steady trickle of vapor from the exhaust. The dead man hunched at the wheel looked ready to start on a long, fast trip to another part of the country.

Graves's Studebaker was parked by the pumps at the filling station. Graves and Taggert were standing beside it and came running when I drove up. Their faces were pale and slick with excitement.

"It was a black limousine," Graves said. "We drove away slow and saw him stop at the corner. I couldn't see his face, but he was wearing a cap and a leather windbreaker."

"He still is."

"Did you see him pass you?" Taggert's voice was so tense he whispered.

"He turned off before he got to me. He's sitting in his car on the next side road with a bullet in his head."

"Good Christ!" Graves cried. "You didn't shoot him, Lew?"

"Somebody else did. A cream convertible came out of the side road a minute after the shot. I think a woman was driving. She headed for L. A. Now, are you sure he got the money?"

"I saw him pick it up."

"He hasn't got it any more; so one of two things happened. It was a heist, or his partners double-crossed him. If he was highjacked, his partners don't get the hundred grand. If they double-crossed him, they'll double-cross us. Either way it's bad for Sampson."

"What do we do now?" Taggert said.

Graves answered him. "We take the wraps off the case. Give the police the go-ahead. Post a reward. I'll see Mrs. Sampson about it."

"One thing, Bert," I said. "We've got to keep this shooting quiet—out of the papers anyway. If highjackers did it, his partners will blame us, and that's the end of Sampson."

"The dirty bastards!" Graves's voice was heavy and grim. "We kept our side of the bargain. If I could get my hands on them—"

"You wouldn't know it. All we have is a dead man in a rented car. You better start with the sheriff; he won't do much, but it's a nice gesture. Then the highway patrol and the F.B.I. Get as many men on it as you can."

I released my emergency brake and let the car roll a few inches. Graves backed away from the window. "Where do you think you're going?"

"On a wild-goose chase. Things look so bad for Sampson I might as well."

It took me down the highway fifty miles to Buenavista. The highway doubled as the town's main street. It was lit by motel and tavern signs and three theater fronts. Two of the three theaters advertised Mexican films. The Mexicans lived

off the land when the canneries were closed. The rest of the
townspeople lived off the Mexicans and the fishing fleet.

I stopped in the middle of the town, in front of an over-
grown cigar store that sold guns, magazines, fishing tackle,
draft beer, stationery, baseball gloves, contraceptives, and
cigars. Two dozen Mexican boys with grease-slicked duck-tail
haircuts were swarming in and out of the store, drawn two
ways by the pinball machines in the back and the girls on the
street. The girls went by in ribbons and paints, cutting the
air with their bosoms. The boys whistled and postured or pretended to be uninterested.

I called one to the curb and asked him where the Corner
was. He conferred with another pachuco. Then they both
pointed south.

"Straight ahead, about five miles, where the road goes down
to White Beach."

"There's a big red sign," the other boy said, stretching out
his arms enthusiastically. "You can't miss it. The Corner."

I thanked them. They bowed and smiled and nodded as
if I had done them a favor.

The sign spelled out "The Corner" in red-neon script on
the roof of a long, low building to the right of the highway.
A black-and-white sign at the intersection beyond it pointed
to White Beach. I parked in the asphalt parking-space beside
the building. There were eight or ten other cars in the lot,
and a trailer truck on the shoulder of the highway. Through
the half-curtained windows I could see a few couples at tables,
a few others dancing.

To the left as I went in was a long bar, totally empty. The
dining-room and dance floor was to the right. I stood at the
entrance as if I was looking for somebody. There weren't

enough dancers to bring the big room to life. Their music came from a jukebox. There was an empty orchestra stand at the back of the room. All that was left of the big war nights were the foot-grained floor, rows of unset rickety tables, odors like drunken memories in the walls, tattered decorations like drunken hopes.

The customers felt the depression in the room. Their faces groped for laughter and enjoyment and couldn't quite get hold of them. None of the faces meant anything to me.

The solitary waitress came up to me. She had dark eyes and a soft mouth, a good body going to seed at twenty. You could read her history in her face and body. She walked carefully as if she had sore feet.

"You want a table, sir?"

"Thanks, I'll sit in the bar. You may be able to help me, though. I'm looking for a man I met at a baseball game. I don't see him."

"What's his name?"

"That's the trouble—I don't know his name. I owe him money on a bet, and he said he'd meet me here. He's a little fellow, about thirty-five, wears a leather windbreaker and a leather cap. Blue eyes, sharp nose." And a hole in his head, sister, a hole in his head.

"I think I know who you mean. His name's Eddie something, or something. He comes in for a drink sometimes, but he hasn't been in tonight."

"He said he'd meet me here. What time does he usually come in?"

"Later than this—around midnight. He drives a truck, don't he?"

"Yeah, a blue truck."

"That's the one," she said. "I seen it in the parking lot. He was in a couple of nights ago, used our phone for a long-distance telephone call. Three nights ago, it was. The boss didn't like it—you never know how much to collect when it runs over three minutes—but Eddie said he'd reverse the charges, so the boss let him go ahead. How much do you owe him, anyway?"

"Plenty. You don't know where he was calling?"

"No. It's none of my business, anyway. Is it any of yours?"

"It's just that I want to get in touch with him. Then I could send him his money."

"You can leave it with the boss if you want to."

"Where's he?"

"Chico, behind the bar."

A man at one of the tables rapped with his glass, and she walked carefully away. I went into the bar.

The bartender's face, from receding hairline to slack jaw, was terribly long and thin. His night of presiding at an empty bar made it seem even longer. "What'll it be?"

"A beer."

His jaw dropped another notch. "Eastern or Western?"

"Eastern."

"That's thirty-five, with the music." His jaw recovered the lost ground. "We provide the music."

"Can I get a sandwich?"

"Sure thing," he said, almost cheerfully. "What kind?"

"Bacon and egg."

"O.K." He signaled the waitress through the open door.

"I'm looking for a guy called Eddie," I said. "The one that phoned me long-distance the other night."

"You from Las Vegas?"

"Just came from there."

"How's business in L. V.?"

"Pretty slow."

"That's too bad," he said happily. "What were you looking for him for?"

"I owe him some money. Does he live around here?"

"Yeah, I think he does. I don't know where, though. He come in once or twice with a blond dame. Probably his wife. He might come in tonight for all I know. Stick around."

"Thanks, I will."

I took my beer to a table beside the window, from which I could watch the parking lot and the main entrance. After a while the waitress brought my sandwich. She lingered even after I paid and tipped her.

"Going to leave the money with the boss?"

"I'm thinking about it. I want to be sure he gets it."

"You must be eaten up with honesty, eh?"

"You know what happens to bookies that don't pay off."

"I sort of thought you was a bookie." She leaned toward me with sudden urgency. "Listen, mister, I got a girl friend, she goes out with an exercise boy, she says he says Jinx is a cert in the third tomorrow. Would you bet it on the nose or across the board?"

"Save your money," I said. "You can't beat them."

"I only bet tip money. This boy, my girl friend's boy friend, he says Jinx is a cert."

"Save it."

Her mouth pursed skeptically. "You're a funny kind of bookie."

"All right." I handed her two ones. "Play Jinx to show."

She looked at me with a scowl of surprise. "Gee, thanks, mister—only I wasn't asking for money."

"It's better than losing your own money," I said.

I hadn't eaten for nearly twelve hours, and the sandwich tasted good. While I was eating it several cars arrived. A party of young people came in laughing and talking, and business picked up at the bar. Then a black sedan rolled into the parking lot, a black Ford sedan with a red police searchlight sticking out like a sore thumb beside the windshield.

The man who got out wore plain clothes as obvious as a baseball umpire's suit, with gun wrinkles over the right hip. I saw his face when he came into the circle of light from the entrance. It was the deputy sheriff from Santa Teresa. I got up quickly and went through the door at the end of the bar into the men's lavatory, locking the door behind me. I lowered the top of the toilet seat and sat down to brood over my lack of foresight. I shouldn't have left the book matches in Eddie something's pocket.

I put in eight or ten minutes reading the inscriptions on the whitewashed walls. "John 'Rags' Latino, Winner 120 Hurdles, Dearborn High School, Dearborn, Mich., 1946." "Franklin P. Schneider, Osage County, Oklahoma, Deaf Mute, Thank you." The rest of them were the usual washroom graffiti interspersed with primitive line drawings.

The naked bulb in the ceiling shone in my eyes. My brain skipped a beat, and I went to sleep sitting up. The room was a whitewashed corridor slanting down into the bowels of the earth. I followed it down to the underground river of filth that ran under the city. There was no turning back. I had to wade the excremental river. Fortunately I had my stilts with me. They carried me untainted, wrapped in cellophane, to the landing on the other side. I tossed my stilts away—they were also crutches—and mounted a chrome-plated escalator that gleamed like the jaws of death. Smoothly and surely it lifted me through all the zones of evil to a rose-embowered gate, which a maid in gingham opened for me, singing Home, Sweet Home.

I stepped out into a stone-paved square, and the gate clanged shut behind me. It was the central square of the city, but I was alone in it. It was very late. Not a streetcar was in sight. A single yellow light shone down on the foot-smoothed pavement. When I moved, my footsteps echoed lonesomely, and on all four sides the hunchbacked tenements muttered like a forest before a storm. The gate clanged shut again, and I opened my eyes.

Something metallic was pounding on the door.

"Open up," the deputy sheriff said. "I know you're in there."

I slipped the bolt and pulled the door wide open. "You in a hurry, officer?"

"So it's you. I thought maybe it was you." His black eyes and heavy lips were bulging with satisfaction. He had a gun in his hand.

"I knew damn well it was you," I said. "I didn't think it was necessary to tell everybody in the place."

"Maybe you had a reason for keeping quiet, eh? Maybe you had a reason for hiding in here when I come in? The sheriff thinks it's an inside job, and he'll want to know what you're doing here."

"This is the guy," the bartender said, at his shoulder. "He said Eddie phoned him in Las Vegas."

"What you got to say to that?" the deputy demanded. He waggled the gun in my face.

"Come in and close the door."

"Yeah? Then put your hands on your head."

"I don't think so."

"Put your hands on your head." The gun poked into my solar plexus. "You carrying a gun?" He started to frisk me with his other hand.

I stepped back out of his reach. "I'm carrying a gun. You can't have it."

He moved toward me again. The door swung closed behind him. "You know what you're doing, eh? Resisting an officer-inperformancehisduty. I got a good mind to put you under arrest."

"You got a good mind, period."

"No cracks from you, jerk. All I want to know is what you're doing here."

"Enjoying myself."

"So you won't talk, eh?" he said, like a comic-book cop. He raised his free hand to slap me.

"Hold it," I said. "Don't lay a finger on me."

"And why not?"

"Because I've never killed a cop. It would be a blot on my record."

Our glances met and deadlocked. His raised hand hung stiff in the air and gradually subsided.

"Now put your gun away," I said. "I don't like being threatened."

"Nobody asked you what you liked," he said, but his fire had gone out. His swarthy face was caught between conflicting emotions: anger and doubt, suspicion and bewilderment.

"I came here for the same reason you did—officer." The word came hard, but I managed to get it out. "I found the book matches in Eddie's pocket—"

"How come you know his name?" he said alertly.

"The waitress told me."

"Yeah? The bartender said he phoned you in Las Vegas."

"I was trying to pump the bartender. Get it? It was a gag. I was trying to be subtle."

"Well, what did you find out?"

."The dead man's name is Eddie, and he drove a truck. He came in here for drinks sometimes. Three nights ago he phoned Las Vegas from here. Sampson was in Las Vegas three nights ago."

"No kidding?"

"I wouldn't kid you, officer, even if I could."

"Jesus," he said, "it all fits in, don't it?"

"I never thought of that," I said. "Thank you very much for pointing it out to me."

He gave me a queer look, but he put away his gun.

chapter **20**   I drove a half a mile down the highway, turned, drove back again, and parked at the inter-section diagonally across from the Corner. The deputy's car was still in the parking lot.

The fog was lifting, dissolving into the sky like milk in water, and blowing out to sea. The expanding horizon only reminded me that Ralph Sampson could be a long way from there—anywhere at all. Starving to death in a mountain cabin, drowned at the bottom of the sea, or wearing a hole in the head like Eddie. The cars went by the roadhouse in both directions, headed for home or headed for brighter lights. In the rear-vision mirror my face was ghostly pale, as if I had caught a little death from Eddie. There were circles under my eyes, and I needed a shave.

A truck came up from the south and passed me slowly. It wheeled into the parking lot of the Corner. The truck was blue and had a closed van. A man jumped down from the cab and shuffled across the asphalt. I knew his rubber-kneed walk, and in the light from the entrance I knew his face. A savage sculptor had hacked it out of stone and smashed it with another stone.

He stopped with a jerk when he saw the black police car. Stopped and turned and ran back to the blue truck. It backed out with a grinding of gears, and turned down the road towards White Beach. When its tail light had dwindled to a red spark, I followed it. The road changed from black-top to gravel, and finally to sand. For two miles I ate his dust.

Where the road came down to the beach between two bluffs, another road crossed it. The lights of the truck turned left and climbed the slope. When they were over the rise and out of sight, I followed them. The road was a single track cut into the side of the hill. From the crest I could see the ocean below to my right. There was a traveling moon in the clouds, which were drifting out to sea. Its light on the black water made a dull lead-foil shine.

The hill flattened out ahead, and the road straightened. I drove on slowly with my lights out. Before I knew it I was abreast of the truck. It was standing in a lane with no lights showing, fifty yards off the road. I kept going.

The road ended abruptly at the bottom of the hill a quarter mile further on. A lane meandered off toward the ocean on the right, but its entrance was blocked by a wooden gate. I turned my car in the dead end and climbed the hill on foot.

A row of eucalyptus trees, ragged against the sky, edged the lane where the truck was standing. I left the road and kept them between me and the truck. The ground was uneven, dotted with clumps of coarse grass. I stumbled more than once. Then space fell open in front of me, and I nearly walked off the edge of the bluff. Far down below, the white surf stroked the beach. The sea looked close enough for a dive, but hard as metal.

Below me to the right there was a white square of light. I climbed and slid down the side of the hill, holding onto the grass to keep from falling. A small building took shape around the light, a white cottage held in a groin of the bluff.

The unblinded window gave me a full view of the single room. I felt for the gun in my holster and approached the window on my hands and knees. There were two people in the room. Neither of them was Sampson.

Puddler was wedged in a chair cut out of a barrel, his broken profile toward me, a bottle of beer in his fist. He was facing a woman on an unmade studio bed against the wall. The gasoline lamp that hung from a rafter in the unplastered ceiling threw a hard white light on her streaked blond hair and her face. It was a thin and harried face, with wide resentful nostrils and a parched mouth. Only the cold brown eyes were lively in it, darting and peering from the puckered skin of their sockets. I moved my head sideways, out of their range.

The room wasn't large, but it seemed to be terribly bare. The pine floor was carpetless, slick with grime. A wooden table piled with dirty dishes stood under the light. Beyond it against the far wall were a two-burner oil stove, a sagging icebox, a rust-mottled sink with a tin pail under it to catch the drip.

The room was so still, the clapboard walls so thin, that I could hear the steady suspiration of the lamp. And Puddler's voice when he said:

"I can't wait here all night, can I? You can't expect me to wait here all night. I got a job to get back to. And I don't like that pollice car setting up there at the Corner."

"That's what you said before. That car don't mean anything."

"I'm saying it again. I should of been back at the Piano already; you know that. Mr. Troy was mad when Eddie didn't show."

"Let him get apoplexy." The woman's voice was sharp and thin like her face. "If he don't like the way Eddie does the job, he can stick it."

"You ain't in no position to talk like that." Puddler looked from side to side of the room. "You didn't talk like that when Eddie come sucking around for a job when he got out of the pen. When he got out of the pen and come sucking around for a job and Mr. Troy give him one—"

"For God's sake! Can't you stop repeating yourself, dim brain?"

His scarred face gathered in folds of hurt surprise. He drew in his head, and his thick neck wrinkled up like a turtle's neck. "That's no way to talk, Marcie."

"You shut your yap about Eddie and the pen." Her voice

bit like a thin knife blade. "How many jails you seen the inside of, dim brain?"

His answer was a tormented bellow. "Lay off me, hear."

"All right then, lay off Eddie."

"Where the hell is Eddie, anyway?"

"I don't know where he is or why, but I know he's got a reason."

"It better be good when he talks to Mr. Troy."

"*Mister* Troy, *Mister* Troy. He's got you hypnotized, hasn't he? Maybe Eddie won't be talking to Mr. Troy."

His small eyes peered at her, trying to read her meaning in her face, and gave up. "Listen, Marcie," he said after a pause. "You can drive the truck."

"The hell you say! I want no part of that racket."

"It's good enough for me. It's good enough for Eddie. You're getting awful fancy-pants since he took you off the street—"

"Shut up or you'll be sorry!" she said. "The trouble with you is you're yellow. You see a patrol car and you wet your pants. So you try to get a woman to take your rap, like any other pimp."

He stood up suddenly, brandishing the bottle. "Lay off me, hear. I don't take nothing from nobody. You was a man, I spoil your face for you, hear." The beer foamed out on the floor and over her knees.

She answered very coolly. "You wouldn't say that in front of Eddie. He'd saw you to pieces, and you know it."

"That little monkey!"

"Yeah, that little monkey! Sit down, Puddler. Everybody knows you're a powerful battler. I'll get you another beer."

She got up and moved across the room, stepping lightly

and furiously like a starved cat. Taking a towel from a nail beside the sink, she dabbed at her beer-stained bathrobe.

"You drive the truck?" Puddler said hopefully.

"Do I have to say everything twice, the same as you? I'm not driving the truck. If you're afraid, let one of them drive."

"Naw, I can't do that. They don't know the road; they get knocked off."

"You're wasting time, then, aren't you?"

"Yeah, I guess so." He moved towards her uncertainly, casting a huge shadow on the floor and wall. "How's about a little something before I go? A little party. Eddie's probably in the sack with somebody. I got plenty what it takes."

She picked up a bread knife from the table, the kind with a wavy cutting edge. "Take it away with you, Puddler, or I'll love you up with this."

"Come on now, Marcie. We could get along." He stood still, keeping his distance.

She gulped to control her rising hysteria, but her voice came out as a scream. "Beat it!" The bread knife moved in the glaring light, pointed at his throat.

"O.K., Marcie. You don't have to get mad." He shrugged his shoulders and turned away with the hurt and helpless look of any rejected lover.

I left the window and started up the hill. Before I reached the top, a door swung open, projecting an oblong of light on the hillside. I froze on my hands and knees. I could see the shadow of my head on the dry grass in front of my face.

Then the door closed, drawing darkness over me. Puddler's shadow came out of the pool of shadows behind the house. He went up the steep lane, scuffing the dust with his feet, and disappeared behind the eucalyptus trees.

I had to choose between him and the blond woman, Marcie. I chose Puddler. Marcie could wait. She'd wait forever before Eddie something came back.

chapter **21** A few miles north of Buenavista the blue truck left the highway, turning off to the right. I stopped to let it get well ahead. A sign at the intersection said "Lookout Road." Before I turned up after it, I switched to my fog lamps. The fog had blown out to sea, but I didn't want Puddler to see the same headlights behind him all the way.

All the way was close to seventy miles, two hours of rough driving through mountains. One five-mile stretch, along a ridge so high that my ears hurt, was as bad as any road I'd driven by daylight: two ruts along a black cliff edge, with dark eternity waiting below each curve. The truck highballed along as if it was safe on rails. I let it get out of sight, switched my lights again, and tried to feel like a new man driving a different car.

We came by a different route into the valley Miranda and I had crossed in the afternoon. On the straight valley road I turned out my car lights entirely and drove by the light of the moon, eked out by memory. I thought I knew where the truck was going. I had to be certain.

On the other side of the valley it climbed into the mountains, up the twisting black-top which led to the Temple in the Clouds. I had to use my lights again to follow it. When

I reached Claude's mailbox the wooden gate beside it had been closed. The truck was far above me, a glowworm crawling up the mountain. Higher still, above the jagged black horizon, the cleared sky was salted with stars. The unclouded moon was motionless among them, a round white hole in the night.

I was tired of waiting, of following people down dark roads and never seeing their faces. So far as I knew, there were only the two of them there, Puddler and Claude. I had a gun—and the advantage of surprise.

I opened the gate and drove through, up the winding lane to the rim of the mesa, and down toward the Temple. Above its white mass there was a faint glow from an interior light. The truck was standing inside the open wire gate, its back doors swinging wide. I parked at the gate and got out.

There was nothing inside the truck but crouched shadows, a wooden bench padded with burlap along each side, the pungent odor of men who have sweated and dried in their clothes.

The ironbound door of the temple creaked open then. Claude came out, a moonlit caricature of a Roman senator. His sandals crunched in the gravel. "Who is that?" he said.

"Archer. Remember me?"

I moved from behind the truck and let him see me. He had an electric lantern in his hand. It shone on the gun in mine.

"What are you doing here?" His beard waggled, but his voice was steady.

"Still looking for Sampson," I said.

As I approached he backed toward the door. "You know he is not here. Was one sacrilege not enough for you?"

"Skip the mumbo jumbo, Claude. Did it ever fool anybody at all?"

"Come in if you must, then," he said. "And I see you must."

He held the door for me and closed it after me. Puddler was standing in the center of the court.

"Get over there with Puddler," I said to Claude.

But Puddler came towards me in a shuffling run. I shot once at his feet. The bullet made a white scar in the stone in front of him and whined into the adobe wall on the other side of the court. Puddler stood still and looked at me.

Claude made a half-hearted try to knock down my gun. I took him in the stomach with my elbow. He doubled up on the pavement.

"Come here," I said to Puddler. "I want to talk to you."

He stayed where he was. Claude sat up hugging his torso and cried out loudly in a Spanish dialect I didn't understand. A door sprang open as if it knew Spanish, on the other side of the court. A dozen men came out. They were small and brown, moving quickly toward me. Their teeth flashed in the moonlight. They came on silently, and I was afraid of them. Because of that, or something else, I held my fire. The brown men looked at the gun and came on anyway.

I clubbed the gun and waited. The first two got bloody scalps. Then they swarmed over me, hung on my arms, kicked my legs from under me, kicked consciousness out of my head. It slid like a disappearing tail light down the dark mountain-side of the world.

I came to fighting. My arms were pinned, my raw mouth kissing cement. I realized after a while that I was fighting myself. My arms were tied behind me, my legs bent up and tied to my wrists. All I could do was rock a little and beat the side of my head against cement. I decided against this policy.

I tried yelling. My skull vibrated like live skin on a drumhead. I couldn't hear my voice above the roar. I gave up yelling. The roar went on in my head, rising higher and higher until it was out of my range, a silent screech. Then the real pain began, pounding my temples in syncopated rhythm like roustabouts driving stakes. I was grateful for any interruption, even Claude.

"The wrath of the god is heavy," he said, above and behind me. "You may not desecrate his temple with impunity."

"Stop gabbling," I said, to the cement. "You'll be up against two kidnapping raps instead of one."

"Bum raps, Mr. Archer." He made a clucking sound, tongue against palate. By straining my neck I could see his gnarled, sandaled feet on the floor near my head.

"You misunderstand the situation," he said, putting on his vocabulary like a garment. "You invaded our retreat by armed force, assaulted me, attacked my friends and disciples—"

I tried to laugh mirthlessly, and succeeded. "Is Puddler one of your disciples? He's a very spiritual type."

"Listen to me, Mr. Archer. We might with perfect justification have killed you in self-defense. Your life is still in our gift."

"Why don't you climb up the chimney and ride away?"

"You fail to understand the seriousness of this—"

"I understand that you're a smelly old crook." I tried to think of subtler insults, but my brain wasn't functioning properly.

He stamped with his heel in my side, just above the kid-

neys. My mouth opened, and my teeth ground on the cement.
No sound came out.

"Think about it," he said.

The light receded and a door slammed. The pain in my
head and body pulsated like a star. Small and remote, then
large and near, then dwindling down to a whirring point, the
tip of a restless drill.

On the threshold of consciousness my mind swarmed with
images from beyond the threshold: uglier faces than I'd seen
in any street, eviller streets than I'd seen in any city. I came
to the empty square in the city's heart. Death lurked behind
the muttering windows, an old whore with sickness under
her paint. A face looked down at me, changing by the second:
Miranda's brown young face sprouting gray hair, Claude's
mouth denuded to become Fay's smile, Fay shrinking down,
all but the great dark eyes, to the Filipino's head, which was
withered by rapid age to the silver head of Troy. Eddie's
bright dead gaze came back again and again, and the Mexican
faces repeated themselves, each one like the other, with flat
black eyes and shining teeth curved downward in a smile of
anger and fear. With my arms roped tight behind me, my
heels pressed into my buttocks, I slid over the threshold into
a bad sleep.

Light against my eyelids brought me back to a closed red
world. I heard a voice above me and kept my eyes closed.
The voice was Troy's soft purr.

"You've made a serious error, Claude. I know this chap,
you see. Now why shouldn't you have told me about his
earlier visit?"

"I didn't think it was important. He was looking for Sampson, that was all. Sampson's daughter was with him." Claude

was speaking naturally for the first time. His voice had lost its orotundity and risen a full octave. He made sounds like a frightened woman.

"You didn't think it was important, eh? I'll tell you just how important it is for you. It means that your usefulness is ended. You can take your brown-skinned doxy and get out."

"This is my place! Sampson said I could live here. You can't order me out."

"I've already done so, Claude. You've bungled your piece of the line, and that means you're finished. Probably the whole thing is finished. We're clearing out of the Temple, and we're not leaving you behind to turn stool pigeon."

"But where can I go? What can I do?"

"Open another store-front church. Go back to Gower Gulch. What you do is no concern of mine."

"Fay won't like this," Claude said hesitantly.

"I don't propose to consult her. And we'll have no more argument, or I'll turn you over to Puddler to argue it out with him. I don't want to do that, because I have one more job for you."

"What is it?" Claude's voice tried to sound eager.

"You can complete the delivery of the current truckload. I'm not at all sure you're competent even for that, but I must risk it. The risk will be largely yours in any case. The ranch foreman will meet you at the southeast entrance to give them safe conduct. Do you know where the southeast entrance is?"

"Yes. Just off the highway."

"Very good. When you've unloaded, drive the truck back to Bakersfield and lose it. Don't try to sell it. Leave it in a parking lot and disappear. Can I trust you to do that?"

"Yes, Mr. Troy. But I have no money."

"Here's a hundred."

"Only a hundred?"

"You're lucky to get that, Claude. You can start now. Tell Puddler I want him when he's finished eating."

"You're not going to let him hurt me, Mr. Troy?"

"Don't be silly. I wouldn't let him disarrange a hair of your filthy head."

Claude's sandals scraped away. This time the light remained. Something pulled at the rope that held my wrists. My hands and forearms were numb, but I could feel the strain in my shoulders.

"Lay off!" The movement of my jaw set off a fit of chattering. I had to clench my teeth to stop it.

"You'll be perfectly all right in a jiffy," Troy said. "They've trussed you up like a fowl for market, haven't they?"

I heard a knife whisper through fiber. The tension in my arms and legs was released. They thudded on the cement like pieces of wood. A terrier chill took hold of the back of my neck and shook me.

"Do get up, old fellow."

"I like it here." Sense was returning to the nerves in my arms and legs, burning like a slow fire.

"You mustn't give way to the sulks, Mr. Archer. I warned you once about my associates. If they've dealt with you rather violently, you must admit that you asked for it. And may I suggest that you sell insurance in a highly unusual way. On a mountaintop, in the very early morning, with a gun in your hand. Among men whose life expectancy is considerably better than yours."

I moved my arms on the pavement and kicked my feet

together. The blood was moving through them now, like coarse hot rope. Troy stepped back in two quick tapping movements.

"The gun in my hand is aimed at the back of your head, Mr. Archer. You may get up slowly, however, if you feel quite able."

I gathered my arms and legs under me and forced my body off the pavement. The room spun and lurched to rest. It was one of the bare cells off the court of the Temple. An electric lantern stood on a bench against one wall. Troy was beside it, as dapper and well groomed as ever, with the same nickel-plated gun.

"I gave you the benefit of the doubt last night," he said. "You've rather disappointed me."

"I'm doing my job."

"It seems to conflict with mine." He moved the gun in his hand as if to punctuate the sentence. "Just what exactly is your job, old man?"

"I'm looking for Sampson."

"Is Sampson missing?"

I looked into his impassive face, trying to judge how much he knew. His face didn't say.

"Rhetorical questions bore me, Troy. The point is that you won't gain anything by pulling a second snatch on top of the first. It will pay you to let me go."

"Are you offering me a deal, my dear fellow? You're rather low on bargaining power, aren't you?"

"I'm not working alone," I said. "The cops are in the Piano tonight. They're watching Fay's. Miranda Sampson will be bringing them here today. No matter what you do to me, your racket is finished. Shoot me, and you're finished."

"Perhaps you overestimate your importance." He smiled carefully. "You wouldn't be considering a percentage of tonight's gross?"

"Wouldn't I?" I was trying to think my way around the gun in his hand. My mind was a little vague. I was putting too much effort into standing up.

"Consider my position," Troy said. "A small-time private eye blunders into my business, not once, but twice in rapid succession. I grin and bear it. Not cheerfully, but I bear it. Instead of killing you, which is my inclination, I offer you a one-third cut of tonight's gross. Seven hundred dollars, Mr. Archer."

"A one-third cut of tonight's gross is thirty-three grand."

"What?" He was startled, and his face showed it.

"You want me to spell it out for you?"

He recovered his poise immediately. "You mentioned thirty-three thousand. That's a rather grandiose estimate."

"One third of a hundred thousand is thirty-three thousand three hundred and thirty-three dollars and thirty-three cents."

"What kind of a shakedown are you trying to pull?" His voice was anxious and harsh. I didn't like all that tension converging on the gun.

"Forget it," I said. "I wouldn't touch your money."

"But I don't understand," he said earnestly. "And you mustn't talk in riddles. It makes me jumpy. It makes my hands nervous." The gun moved in illustration.

"Don't you know what goes on, Troy? I thought you knew the angles."

"Assume that I don't know anything. And talk fast."

"Read it in the papers."

"I said talk fast." He raised the gun and let me look into its eye. "Tell me about Sampson and a hundred grand."

"Why should I tell you your business? You kidnapped Sampson two days ago."

"Go on."

"Your driver picked up the hundred grand last night. Wasn't it enough?"

"Puddler did that?" His impassivity had gone for good. A new expression had taken charge of his face, a killer's expression, cruel and intent.

He went to the door and opened it, holding the gun between us. "Puddler!" His voice rose high and cracked.

"The other driver," I said. "Eddie."

"You're lying, Archer."

"All right. Wait for the cops to come and tell you in person. They know by now who Eddie was working for."

"Eddie hasn't the brains."

"Enough brains for a fall guy."

"What do you mean?"

"Eddie's in the morgue."

"Who killed him? Coppers?"

"Maybe you did," I said slowly. "A hundred grand is a lot of money to a small-timer."

He let it pass. "What happened to the money?"

"Somebody shot Eddie and took it away. Somebody in a cream-colored convertible."

Those three words hit him behind the eyes and turned them blank for an instant. I moved to my right and swatted his gun with the palm of my left hand. It spun to the floor without discharging, and slid to the open door.

Puddler was in at the door and on the gun before me. I backed away.

"Do I let him have it, Mr. Troy?"

Troy was shaking his injured hand. It fluttered like a white moth in the circle of light from the lantern.

"Not now," he said. "We've got to clear out of here, and we don't want to leave a mess behind us. Take him to the pier on the Rincon. Use his car. Hold him there until I send word. You follow me?"

"I get it, Mr. Troy. Where are you going to be?"

"I don't quite know. Is Betty at the Piano tonight?"

"Not when I left."

"Do you know where she lives?"

"Naw—she moved the last couple weeks. Somebody lent her a cabin somewheres, I don't know where—"

"Is she driving the same car?"

"The convertible? Yeah. She was last night, anyway."

"I see," Troy said. "I'm surrounded by fools and knaves as usual. They can't keep their heads out of trouble, can they? We'll show them trouble, Puddler."

"Yessir."

"Move," Troy said to me.

chapter **22** They marched me out to my car. Troy's Buick was standing beside it. The truck was gone. Claude and the brown men were gone. It was still black night, with the moon at its lower edge now.

Puddler brought a coil of rope from the shack beside the adobe.

"Put your hands behind you," Troy said to me.

I kept my hands at my sides.

"Put your hands behind you."

"So far I've been doing my job," I said. "If you push me around some more, I'll have a grudge against you."

"You talk a great fight," Troy said. "Quiet him, Puddler."

I turned to face Puddler, not fast enough. His fist struck the nape of my neck. Pain whistled through my body like splintered glass, and the night fell on me solidly again. Then I was on a road. The road was crowded with traffic. I was responsible for the occupants of every car. I had to write a report on each, giving age, occupation, hobby, religion, bank balance, sexual proclivities, politics, crimes, and favorite eating places. The passengers changed cars frequently, like people playing musical chairs. The cars changed numbers and color. My pen ran out of ink. A blue truck picked me up and changed to funeral black. Eddie was at the wheel, and I let him drive. I was planning to kill a man.

The plan was half complete when I came to. I was wedged on the floor of my car between the front and back seats. The floor was vibrating with motion, and the pain in my head kept time. My hands were bound behind me again. Puddler's wide back was in the front seat, outlined by the reflection of the headlights. I couldn't get to my feet, and I couldn't reach him.

I tried to work my hands loose from the rope, twisting and pulling until my wrists were raw and my clothes were wet. The rope held out better than I did. I threw my plan away and started another.

By dark untraveled roads we came down out of the mountains and back to the sea. He parked the car under a tarpaulin stretched on poles. As soon as the engine died I could hear the waves below us beating on the sand. He lifted me out by my coat collar and set me on my feet. I noticed that he pocketed my ignition key.

"Don't make no noise," he said, "unless you want it again."

"You've got a lot of guts," I said. "It takes a lot of guts to hit a man from behind while somebody else holds a gun on him."

"You shut up." He spread his fingers across my face and hooked them downward. They tasted of sweat, as rank as a horse's.

"It takes a lot of guts," I said, "to push a man in the face when his hands are tied behind him."

"You shut up." he said. "I shut you up for good."

"Mr. Troy wouldn't like that."

"You shut up. Get moving." He put his hands on my shoulders, turned me, and pushed me out from under the tarpaulin.

I was at the shore end of a long pier that was built out over the water on piles. There were oil derricks on the skyline behind me, but no lights. No movement but the sea's, and the systole and diastole of an oil pump at the end of the pier. We walked toward it in single file, with Puddler at the rear. The planks of the footwalk were warped and badly put together. Black water gleamed in the cracks.

When we were about a hundred yards from shore I made out the pump at the end of the pier, rising and falling like a mechanical teeter-totter. There was a tool shed beside it, nothing but ocean beyond.

Puddler unlocked the door of the shed, lifted a lantern off a nail, and lit it.

"Sit down, mug." He swung the lantern toward a heavy

bench that stood against the wall. There was a vise at one end of the bench and a few tools scattered along it: pincers, wrenches of various sizes, a rusty file.

I sat down on a clear space. Puddler shut the door and set the lantern on an oil drum. Lit from below by the yellow flaring light, his face was barely human. It was low-browed and prognathous like a Neanderthal man's, heavy and forlorn, without thought. It wasn't fair to blame him for what he did. He was a savage accidentally dropped in the steel-and-concrete jungle, a trained beast of burden, a fighting machine. But I blamed him. I had to. I had to take what he'd handed me or find a way to hand it back to him.

"You're in a rather unusual position," I said.

He didn't hear me, or refused to answer. He leaned against the door, a thick stump of a man blocking my way. I listened to the thump and creak of the pump outside, the water lapping below against the piling. And I thought over the things I knew about Puddler.

"You're in a rather unusual position," I said again.

"Button your lip."

"Acting as jailer, I mean. It's usually the other way around, isn't it? You sit in the cell while somebody else watches you."

"I said button your lip."

"How many jails you seen the inside of, dim brain?"

"Fa Christ sake!" he yelled. "I warned you." He slouched toward me.

"It takes a lot of guts," I said, "to threaten a man when his hands are tied behind him."

His open hand stung my face.

"The trouble with you is you're yellow," I said. "Just like

Marcie said. You're even afraid of Marcie, aren't you, Puddler?"

He stood there blinking, overshadowing me. "I kill you, hear, you talk like that to me. I kill you, hear." The words came out disjointed, moving too fast for his laboring mouth. A bubble of saliva formed at one corner.

"But Mr. Troy wouldn't like that. He told you to keep me safe, remember? There's nothing you can do to me, Puddler."

"Beat your ears off," he said. "I beat your ears off."

"Not if my hands were free, you poor palooka."

"Who you calling palooka?" He drew back his hand again.

"You fifth-rate bum," I said. "You has-been. Down-and-outer. Hit a man when he's tied—it's all you're good for."

He didn't hit me. He took a clasp knife out of his pocket and opened it. His little eyes were red and shining. His whole mouth was wet with saliva now.

"Stand up," he said. "I show you who's a bum."

I turned my back to him. He cut the ropes on my wrists and snapped the knife shut. Then he whirled me toward him and met me with a quick right cross that took away the feeling from my face. I knew I was no match for him. I kicked him in the stomach, and he went to the other side of the room.

While he was coming back I picked up the file from the bench. Its point was blunt, but it would do. I clinched with him. Holding the file near the point in my right hand, I cut him across the forehead with it from temple to temple. He backed away from me. "You cut me," he said incredulously.

"Pretty soon you won't be able to see, Puddler." A Finnish sailor on the San Pedro docks had taught me how Baltic knife-fighters blind their opponents.

"I kill you yet." He came at me like a bull.

I went to the floor and came up under him, jabbing with the file where it would hurt him. He bellowed and went down. I made for the door. He came after me and caught me in the opening. We staggered the width of the pier and fell into space. I took a quick breath before we struck. We went down together. Puddler fought me violently, but his blows were cushioned by the water. I hooked my fingers in his belt and held on.

He threshed and kicked like a terrified animal. I saw his air come out, the silver bubbles rising through the black water to the surface. I held on to him. My lungs were straining for air, my chest was collapsing. The contents of my head were slowing and thickening. And Puddler wasn't struggling any more.

I had to let go of him to reach the surface in time. One deep breath, and I went down after him. My clothes hampered me, and the shoes were heavy on my feet. I went down through strata of increasing cold until my ears were aching with the pressure of the water. Puddler was out of reach and out of sight. I tried six times before I gave him up. The key to my car was in his trousers pocket.

When I swam to shore my legs wouldn't hold me up. I had to crawl out of reach of the surf. It was partly physical exhaustion and partly fear. I was afraid of what was behind me in the cold water.

I lay in the sand until my heartbeat slowed. When I got to my feet the derricks on the horizon were sharply outlined against a lightening sky. I climbed the bank to the shelter where my car was and turned on the lights.

There was a piece of copper wire attached to one of the poles that held the tarpaulin. I pulled it loose and wired my ignition terminals under the dash. The engine started on the first try.

chapter **23**   The sun was over the mountains when I reached Santa Teresa. It put an edge on everything, each leaf and stone and blade of grass. From the canyon road the Sampson house looked like a toy villa built of sugar cubes. Closer up I could feel its massive silence, which dominated the place when I stopped the car. I had to unwire the ignition to cut the motor.

Felix came to the service entrance when I knocked. "Mr. Archer?"

"Is there any doubt about it?"

"You were in an accident, Mr. Archer?"

"Apparently. Is my bag still in the storeroom?" I had fresh clothes in it, and a duplicate set of car keys.

"Yes, sir. There are contusions on your face, Mr. Archer. Should I call a doctor?"

"Don't bother. I could do with a shower, though, if there's one handy."

"Yes, sir. I have a shower over the garage."

He led me to his quarters and brought my bag. I showered and shaved in the dinky bathroom, and changed my sea-sodden clothes. It was all I could do not to stretch out on the unmade bed in his neat little cell of a room and let the case go hang.

When I returned to the kitchen he was setting a tray with a silver breakfast set. "Do you want something to eat, sir?"

"Bacon and eggs, if possible."

He bobbed his round head. "So soon as I have finished with this, sir."

"Who's the tray for?"

"Miss Sampson, sir."

"So early?"

"She will breakfast in her room."

"Is she all right?"

"I do not know, sir. She had a very little sleep. It was past midnight when she came home."

"From where?"

"I do not know, sir. She left at the same time as you and Mr. Graves."

"Driving herself?"

"Yes, sir."

"What car?"

"The Packard convertible."

"Let's see, that's the cream one, isn't it?"

"No, sir. It is red. Bright scarlet. She drove over two hundred miles in the time she was gone."

"You keep a pretty close watch on the family, don't you, Felix?"

He smiled blandly. "It is one of my duties to check the cars for gas and oil, sir, since we have no regular chauffeur."

"But you don't like Miss Sampson very well?"

"I am devoted to her, sir." His opaque black eyes were their own mask.

"Do they give you a rough time, Felix?"

"No, sir. But my family is well known on Samar. I have come to the United States to attend the California Poly-technic College when I am able to do this. I resent Mr.

Graves's assumption that I am suspect because of the color of my skin. The gardeners also resent it for themselves."

"You're talking about last night?"

"Yes, sir."

"I don't think he meant it that way."

Felix smiled blandly.

"Is Mr. Graves here now?"

"No, sir. He is at the sheriff's office, I think. If you will excuse me, sir?" He hoisted the tray to his shoulder.

"You know the number? And do you have to say 'sir' every second word?"

"No, sir," he said with mild irony. "23665."

I dialed the number from the butler's pantry and asked for Graves. A sleepy deputy called him.

"Graves speaking." His voice was hoarse and tired.

"This is Archer."

"Where in God's name have you been?"

"I'll tell you later. Any trace of Sampson?"

"Not yet, but we've made some progress. I'm working with a major case squad from the F.B.I. We wired the classification of the dead man's prints to Washington, and we got an answer about an hour ago. He's in the F.B.I. files with a long record. Name's Eddie Lassiter."

"I'll be over as soon as I eat. I'm at the Sampson place."

"Perhaps you'd better not." He lowered his voice. "The sheriff's peeved at you for running out last night. I'll come there." He hung up, and I opened the door to the kitchen.

Bacon was making cheerful noises in a pan. Felix transferred it to a warming-dish, inserted bread in the toaster beside the stove, broke the eggs in the hot grease, poured me a cup of coffee from a steaming Silex maker.

I sat down at the kitchen table and gulped the scalding coffee. "Are all the phones in the house on the same line?"

"No, sir. The phones in the front of the house are on a different line from the servants' phones. Do you wish your eggs turned over, Mr. Archer?"

"I'll take them the way they are. Which ones are connected with the phone in the pantry?"

"The one in the linen closet and the one in the guest cottage above the house. Mr. Taggert's cottage."

Between mouthfuls I asked him: "Is Mr. Taggert there now?"

"I do not know, sir. I think I heard him drive in during the night."

"Go and make sure, will you?"

"Yes, sir." He left the kitchen by the back door.

A car drove up a minute later, and Graves came in. He had lost some of his momentum, but he still moved quickly. His eyes were red-rimmed.

"You look like hell, Lew."

"I just came from there. Did you bring the dope on Lassiter?"

"Yeah."

He took a teletype flimsy out of his inside pocket and handed it to me. My eye skipped down the closely printed sheet.

Brought before Children's Court, New York, March 29, 1923, father's complaint, truancy. Committed to New York Catholic Protectory, April 4, 1923. Released August 5, 1925. . . . Brooklyn Special Sessions Court, January 9, 1928, charged with bicycle theft. Received suspended sentence and placed on probation. Discharged from probation November 12, 1929. . . . Arrested May 17, 1932, and charged with possession of a stolen money order. Case dismissed for lack of evidence on recommendation U. S. Attorney. . . . Arrested for car theft October 5, 1936, sentenced to 3 years in Sing Sing. . . . Arrested with sister Betty Lassiter by agents of the U. S. Narcotics Bureau, April 23, 1943. Convicted of selling one ounce of cocaine, May 2, 1943, sentenced to year and a day in Leavenworth. . . . Arrested August 3, 1944, for participating in holdup of General Electric payroll truck. Pleaded guilty, sentenced to 5 to 10 years in Sing Sing. Released on parole September 18, 1947. Broke parole and disappeared, December 1947.

Those were the high points in Eddie's record, the dots in the dotted line that marked his course from a delinquent childhood to a violent death. Now it was just as if he had never been born.

Felix said at my shoulder: "Mr. Taggert is in his cottage, sir."

"Is he up?"

"Yes, he is dressing."

"How about some breakfast?" Graves said.

"Yes, sir."

Graves turned to me. "Is there anything useful in it?"

"Just one thing, and it isn't nailed down. Lassiter had a sister named Betty who was arrested with him on a narcotics charge. There's a woman named Betty in Los Angeles with narcotics in her record, a pianist in Tróy's clipjoint. She calls herself Betty Fraley."

"Betty Fraley!" Felix said from the stove.

"This doesn't concern you," Graves told him unpleasantly.

"Wait a minute," I said. "What about Betty Fraley, Felix? Do you know her?"

"I do not know her, no, but I have seen her records, in Mr. Taggert's cottage. I have noticed the name when I dusted there."

"Are you telling the truth?" Graves said.

"Why should I lie, sir?"

"We'll see what Taggert has to say about that." Graves got to his feet.

"Wait a minute, Bert." I put my hand on his arm, which was hard with tension. "Bulldozing won't get us anywhere. Even if Taggert has the woman's records, it doesn't have to mean anything. We're not even certain she's Lassiter's sister. And maybe he's a collector."

"He has quite a large collection," Felix said.

Graves was stubborn. "I think we should take a look at it."

"Not now. Taggert may be as guilty as hell, but we won't get Sampson back by being blunt about it. Wait until Taggert isn't there. Then I'll look over his records."

Graves let me pull him back into his seat. He stroked his closed eyelids with his fingertips. "This case is the wildest mess I've ever seen or heard of," he said.

"It is." Graves only knew the half of it. "Is the general alarm out for Sampson?"

He opened his eyes. "Since ten o'clock last night. We've alerted the highway patrol and the F.B.I., and every police department and county sheriff between here and San Diego."

"You'd better get on the phone," I said, "and put out another state-wide alarm. This time for Betty Fraley. Take in the whole Southwest."

He smiled ironically, with his heavy jaw thrust out. "Doesn't that fall under the category of bluntness?"

"In this case I think it's necessary. If we don't get to Betty fast there'll be somebody there ahead of us. Dwight Troy is gunning for her."

He gave me a curious look. "Where do you get your information, Lew?"

"I got that the hard way. I talked to Troy himself last night."

"He is mixed up in this, then?"

"He is now. I think he wants the hundred grand for himself, and I think he knows who has it."

"Betty Fraley?" He took a notebook out of his pocket.

"That's my guess. Black hair, green eyes, regular features, five foot two or three, between twenty-five and thirty, probable cocaine addict, thin but well stacked, and pretty if you like to play with reptiles. Wanted on suspicion of the murder of Eddie Lassiter."

He glanced up sharply from his writing. "Is that another guess, Lew?"

"Call it that. Will you put it on the wires?"

"Right away." He started across the room to the butler's pantry.

"Not that phone, Bert. It's connected with the one in Taggert's cottage."

He stopped and turned to me with a shadow of grief on his face. "You seem pretty sure that Taggert's our man."

"Would it break your heart if he was?"

"Not mine," he said, and turned away. "I'll use the phone in the study."

chapter **24**   *I waited in the hall at the front of* the house until Felix came to tell me that Taggert was eating breakfast in the kitchen. He led me around the back of the garages, up a path that became a series of low stone steps climbing the side of the hill. When we came within sight of the guest cottage, he left me.

It was a one-story white frame house perched among trees with its back to the hillside. I opened the unlocked door and went in. The living-room was paneled in yellow pine and furnished with easy chairs, a radio-phonograph, a large refectory table covered with magazines and piles of records. The view through the big western window took in the whole estate and the sea to the horizon.

The magazines on the table were *Jazz Record* and *Downbeat*. I went through the records and albums one by one, Decca and Bluebird and Asch, twelve-inch Commodores and Blue Notes. There were many names I had heard of: Fats Waller, Red Nichols, Lux Lewis, Mary Lou Williams—and titles I never had heard of: *Numb Fumblin'* and *Viper's Drag, Night Life, Denapas Parade.* But no Betty Fraley.

I was at the door on my way to talk to Felix when I remembered the black disks skipping out to sea the day before. A few minutes after I saw them, Taggert had come through the house in bathing trunks.

Avoiding the house, I headed for the shore. From the

glassed-in pergola on the edge of the bluff a long flight of concrete steps descended the cliff diagonally to the beach. There was a bath house with a screened veranda at the foot of the steps, and I went in. I found a rubber-and-plate-glass diving mask hanging on a nail in one of the bathhouse cubicles. I stripped to my shorts and adjusted the mask to my head.

A fresh offshore breeze was driving in the waves and blowing off their crests in spray before they broke. The morning sun was hot on my back, the dry sand warm against the soles of my feet. I stood for a minute in the zone of wet brown sand just above the reach of the waves and looked at them. The waves were blue and sparkling, curved as gracefully as women, but I was afraid of them. The sea was cold and dangerous. It held dead men.

I waded in slowly, pulled the mask down over my face, and pushed off. About fifty yards from shore, beyond the surf, I turned on my back and breathed deeply through my mouth. The rise and fall of the swells, and the extra oxygen, made me a little dizzy. Through the misted glass the blue sky seemed to be spinning over my head. I ducked under water to clear the glass, surface-dived, and breast-stroked to the bottom.

It was pure white sand broken by long brown ribs of stone. The sand was roiled a little by the movement of the water, but not enough to spoil the visibility. I zigzagged forty or fifty feet along the bottom and found nothing but a couple of undersized abalones clinging to a rock. I kicked off and went to the surface for air.

When I raised the mask I saw that a man was watching me from the cliff. He ducked down behind the wild-cherry windbreak by the pergola, but not before I had recognized

Taggert. I took several deep breaths and dived again. When I came up, Taggert had disappeared.

On the third dive I found what I was looking for, an unbroken black disk half buried in the sand of the bottom. Holding the record against my chest, I turned on my back and kicked myself to shore. I took it into the shower and washed and dried it with tender care, like a mother with an infant.

Taggert was on the veranda when I came out of the dressing-rooms. He was sitting in a canvas chair with his back to the screen door. In flannel slacks and a white T-shirt, he looked very young and brown. The black hair on his small head was carefully brushed.

He gave me a boyish grin that didn't touch his eyes. "Hello there, Archer. Have a nice swim?"

"Not bad. The water's a little cold."

"You should have used the pool. It's always warmer."

"I prefer the ocean. You never know what you're going to find. I found this."

He looked at the record in my hands as if he was noticing it for the first time. "What is it?"

"A record. Somebody seems to have scraped the labels off and thrown it in the sea. I wonder why."

He took a step toward me, long and noiseless on the grass rug. "Let me see."

"Don't touch it. You might break it."

"I won't break it."

He reached for it. I jerked it out of his reach. His hand grasped air.

"Stand back," I said.

"Give it to me, Archer."

"I don't think so."

"I'll take it away from you."

"Don't do that," I said. "I think I can break you in two."

He stood and looked at me for ten long seconds. Then he turned on the grin again. The boyish charm was very slow in coming. "I was just kidding, man. But I'd still like to know what's on the bloody thing."

"So would I."

"Let's play it then. There's a portable player here." He moved around me to the table in the center of the veranda and opened a square fiber box.

"I'll play it," I said.

"That's right—you're afraid I'll break it." He went back to his chair and sat down, stretching his legs in front of him.

I cranked the machine and placed the record on the turntable. Taggert was smiling expectantly. I stood and watched him, waiting for a sign, a wrong move. The handsome boy didn't fit into the system of fears I had. He didn't fit into any pattern I knew.

The record was scratched and tired. A single piano began to beat, half drowned in surface noise. Three or four hackneyed boogie chords were laid down and repeated. Then the right hand wove through them, twisting them alive. The first chords multiplied and built themselves around the room. The place they made was half jungle, half machine. The right hand moved across it and back again like something being chased. Chased through an artificial jungle by the shadow of a giant.

"You like it?" Taggert said.

"Within limits. If the piano was a percussion instrument it would be first-rate."

"But that's just the point. It is a percussion instrument if you want to use it that way."

The record ended, and I turned it off. "You seem to be interested in boogie-woogie. You wouldn't know who made this record?"

"I wouldn't, no. The style could be Lux Lewis."

"I doubt it. It sounds more like a woman's playing."

He frowned in elaborate concentration. His eyes were small in his head. "I don't know of any woman who can play like that."

"I know of one. I heard her in the Wild Piano night before last. Betty Fraley."

"I never heard of her," he said.

"Come off it, Taggert. This is one of her records."

"Is it?"

"You should know. You tossed it in the sea. Now why would you do that?"

"The question doesn't arise, because I didn't do it. I wouldn't dream of throwing good records away."

"I think you dream a great deal, Taggert. I think you've been dreaming about a hundred thousand dollars."

He shifted slightly in his chair. His stretched-out pose had stiffened and lost its air of casualness. If someone had lifted him by the nape of the neck, his legs would have stayed as they were, straight out before him in the air.

"Are you suggesting that I kidnapped Sampson?"

"Not personally. I'm suggesting that you conspired to do it—with Betty Fraley and her brother Eddie Lassiter."

"I never heard of them, either of them." He drew a deep breath.

"You will. You'll meet one of them in court, and hear about the other."

"Now just a minute," he said. "You're going too fast for me. Is this because I threw those records away?"

"This is your record, then?"

"Sure." His voice was vibrantly frank. "I admit I had some of Betty Fraley's records. I got rid of them last night when I heard you talking to the police about the Wild Piano."

"You also listen to other people's telephone conversations?"

"It was purely accidental. I overheard you when I was trying to make a phone call of my own."

"To Betty Fraley?"

"I told you I don't know her."

"Excuse me," I said. "I thought perhaps you phoned her last night to give her the green light on the murder."

"The murder?"

"The murder of Eddie Lassiter. You don't have to act so surprised, Taggert."

"But I don't know anything about these people."

"You knew enough to throw away Betty's records."

"I'd heard of her, that's all. I knew she played at the Wild Piano. When I heard the police were interested in the place, I got rid of her records. You know how unreasonable they can be about circumstantial evidence."

"Don't try to kid me the way you've kidded yourself," I said. "An innocent man would never have thought of throwing those records away. People all over the country have them, haven't they?"

"That's just my point. There's nothing incriminating about them."

"But you thought there was, Taggert. You'd have had no reason to think of them as evidence against you, if you really weren't in this thing with Betty Fraley. And it happens that you threw them in the sea a good many hours before you heard my phone call—before Betty was ever mentioned in connection with this case."

"Maybe I did," he said. "But you're going to have a time hanging anything on me on the basis of those records."

"I'm not going to try to. They put me on to you and served their purpose. So let's forget about the records and talk about something important." I sat down in a wicker chair across the veranda from him.

"What do you want to talk about?" He still had perfect control. His puzzled smile was natural, and his voice was easy. Only his muscles gave him away, bunched at the shoulders, quivering in the thighs.

"Kidnapping," I said. "We'll leave the murder till later. Kidnapping is just about as serious in this state. I'll give you my version of the kidnapping, and then I'll listen to yours. A great many people will be eager to listen to yours."

"Too bad. I haven't any version."

"I have. I'd have seen it sooner if I hadn't happened to like you. You had more opportunity than anyone, and more motive. You resented Sampson's treatment of you. You resented all the money he had. You hadn't much yourself—"

"Still haven't," he said.

"You should be well fixed for the present. Half of the hundred thousand is fifty thousand. The very temporary present."

He spread his hands humorously. "Am I carrying it with me?"

"You're not that dull," I said. "But you're dull enough. You've acted like a rube, Taggert. The city slickers sucked you in and used you. You'll probably never see your half of the hundred grand."

"You promised me a story," he said smoothly. He was going to be hard to break down.

I showed him my best card. "Eddie Lassiter phoned you the night before you flew Sampson out of Las Vegas."

"Don't tell me you're psychic, Archer. You said the man was dead." But there was a new white line around Taggert's mouth.

"I'm psychic enough to tell you what you said to Eddie. You told him you'd be flying into Burbank about three o'clock the next day. You told him to rent a black limousine and wait for your phone call from the Burbank airport. When Sampson phoned the Valerio for a limousine, you canceled the call and sent for Eddie instead. The operator at the Valerio thought it was Sampson calling back. You do a pretty good imitation of him, don't you?"

"Go on," he said. "I've always been fond of fantasy."

"When Eddie turned up at the front of the airport in the rented car, Sampson got in as a matter of course. He had no reason to suspect anything. You had him so drunk he wouldn't notice the difference in drivers—so drunk that even a little guy like Eddie could handle him when they got to a private place. What did Eddie use on him, Taggert? Chloroform?"

"This is supposed to be your story," he said. "Is your imagination getting tired?"

"The story belongs to both of us. That canceled telephone call was important, Taggert. It was the thing that tied you into the story in the first place. Nobody else could have known that Sampson was going to phone the Valerio. Nobody else knew when Sampson was going to fly in from Nevada. Nobody else was in a position to give Eddie the tip-off the night before. Nobody else could have made all the arrangements and run them off on schedule."

"I never denied I was at the airport with Sampson. There were a few hundred other people there at the same time. You're hipped on circumstantial evidence, like any other cop. And this business of the records isn't even circumstantial evidence. It's a circular argument. You haven't got anything on Betty Fraley, and you haven't proved any connection between us. Hundreds of collectors have her records."

His voice was still cool and clear, bright with candor, but he was worried. His body was hunched and tense, as if I had forced him into a narrow space. And his mouth was turning ugly.

"It shouldn't be hard to prove a connection." I said. "You must have been seen together at one time or another. And wasn't it you that called her the other night when you saw me in the Valerio with Fay Estabrook? You weren't really looking for Sampson at the Wild Piano, were you? You were going to see Betty Fraley. You put me off when you pulled Puddler out of my hair. I thought you were on my side. So much so that I put it down to stupidity when you fired at the blue truck. You were warning Eddie off, weren't you, Taggert? I'd call you a smart boy if you hadn't dirtied your hands with kidnapping and murder. Stupidity like that cancels out the smartness."

"If you're through calling me names," he said, "we'll get down to business."

He was still sitting quietly in the canvas chair, but his hand came up from beside him with a gun. It was the .32 target pistol I had seen before, a light gun but heavy enough to make my stomach crawl.

"Keep your hands on your knees," he said.

"I didn't think you'd give up so easily."

"I haven't given up. I'm simply guaranteeing my freedom of action."

"Shooting me won't guarantee it. It'll guarantee something else. Death by gas. Put your gun away and we'll talk this over."

"There's nothing to talk over."

"You're wrong, as usual. What do you think I'm trying to do in this case?"

He didn't answer. Now that the gun was in his hand, ready for violence, his face was smooth and relaxed. It was the face of a new kind of man, calm and unfrightened, because he laid no special value on human life. Boyish and rather innocent, because he could do evil almost without knowing it. He was the kind of man who had grown up and found himself in war.

"I'm trying to find Sampson," I said. "If I can get him back, nothing else counts."

"You've gone about it the wrong way, Archer. You forgot what you said last night: if anything happens to the people that kidnapped Sampson, it's the end of him."

"Nothing has happened to you—yet."

"Nothing has happened to Sampson."

"Where is he?"

"Where he won't be found until I want him to be."

"You have your money. Let him go."

"I intended to, Archer. I was going to turn him loose to-day. But that will have to be postponed—indefinitely. If anything happens to me, it's good-bye Sampson."

"We can reach an understanding."

"No," he said. "I couldn't trust you. We have to get clear away. Don't you see that you've spoilt it? You have the power to spoil things, but you haven't the power to guarantee that we'll get clear. There's nothing I can do with you but this."

He glanced down at the gun, which was pointed at the middle of my body, then casually back at me. Any second he could shoot, without preparation, without anger. All he had to do was pull the trigger.

"Wait," I said. My throat was tight. My skin felt desiccated, and I wanted to sweat. My hands were clutching my knees.

"We don't want to stretch this out." He stood up and moved toward me.

I shifted the weight of my body in the chair. One shot wouldn't kill me, unless my luck was bad. Between the first and the second I could reach him. As I drew back my feet I talked rapidly.

"If you'll give me Sampson, I can guarantee that I won't try to hold you and I won't talk. You'll have to take your chances with the others. Kidnapping is like other business enterprises: you have to take your chances."

"I'm taking them," he said, "but not on you."

His rigid arm came up with the gun at the end like a hollow blue finger. I looked sideways, away from the direction I was going to move in. I was halfway out of the chair when the gun went off. Taggert was listless when I got to him. The gun slid out of his hand.

Another gun had spoken. Albert Graves was in the doorway with the twin of Taggert's pistol in his hand. He poked the end of his little finger through a round hole in the screen.

"Too bad," he said, "but it had to be done."

The water ran down my face.

chapter **25**   I caught Taggert's limber *body* as it fell, and laid it out on the grass rug. The dark eyes were open and glistening. They didn't react to the touch of my fingertips. The round hole in the right temple was bloodless. A death mark like a little red birthmark, and Taggert was thirty dollars' worth of organic chemicals shaped like a man.

Graves was standing over me. "He's dead?"

"He didn't fall down in a fit. You did a quick, neat job."

"It was you or Taggert."

"I know," I said. "I don't like to quibble. But I wish you'd shot the gun out of his hand or smashed the elbow of his gun arm."

"I couldn't trust myself to do that kind of shooting any more. I got out of practice in the army." His mouth twisted wryly, and one of his eyebrows went up. "You're a carping son of a bitch, Lew. I save your life, and you criticize the method."

"Did you hear what he said?"

"Enough. He kidnapped Sampson."

"But he wasn't alone. His friends aren't going to like this. They'll take it out on Sampson."

"Sampson is alive, then?"

"According to Taggert he is."

"Who are these others?"

"Eddie Lassiter was one. Betty Fraley is another. There may be more. You'll be calling the police about this shooting?"

"Naturally."

"Tell them to keep it quiet."

"I'm not ashamed of it, Lew," he told me sharply, "though you seem to think I should be. It had to be done, and you know the law on it as well as I do."

"Look at it from Betty Fraley's point of view. It won't be the legal one. When she hears what you've done to her sidekick she'll beeline for Sampson and make a hole in *his* head. Why should she bother keeping him alive? She's got the money—"

"You're right," he said. "We've got to keep it out of the papers and off the radio."

"And we've got to find her before she gets to Sampson. Watch yourself, too, Bert. She's dangerous, and I have an idea that she was gone on Taggert."

"Her, too?" he said, and after a pause: "I wonder how Miranda's going to take it."

"Pretty hard. She liked him, didn't she?"

"She had a crush on him. She's a romantic, you know, and awfully young. Taggert had the things she thought she wanted, youth and good looks and a hell of a combat record. This thing is going to shock her."

"I don't shock easily," I said, "but it took me by surprise.

I thought he was a pretty sound kid, a little self-centered but solid."

"You don't know the type like I do," Graves said. "I've seen this same thing happen to other boys, not to such an extreme degree, of course, but the same thing. They went out of high school into the army or the air corps and made good in a big way. They were officers and gentlemen with high pay, an even higher opinion of themselves, and all the success they needed to keep it blown up. War was their element, and when the war was finished, they were finished. They had to go back to boys' jobs and take orders from middle-aged civilians. Handling pens and adding machines instead of flight sticks and machine guns. Some of them couldn't take it and went bad. They thought the world was their oyster and couldn't understand why it had been snatched away from them. They wanted to snatch it back. They wanted to be free and happy and successful without laying any foundation for freedom or happiness or success. And there's the hangover."

He looked down at the new corpse on the floor. Its eyes were still open, gazing up through the roof at the empty sky. I bent down and closed them.

"We're becoming very elegiac," I said. "Let's get out of here."

"In a minute." He laid his hand on my arm. "I want you to do me a favor, Lew."

"What is it?"

He spoke with diffidence. "I'm afraid if I tell Miranda about this, she won't see it the way it happened. You know what I mean—she might blame me."

"You want me to tell her?"

"I know it's not your baby, but I'd appreciate it."

"I can do that," I said. "I suppose you did save my life."

Mrs. Kromberg was running a vacuum cleaner in the big front room. She glanced up when I entered, and switched it off. "Mr. Graves find you all right?"

"He found me."

Her face sharpened. "Anything wrong?"

"It's over now. Do you know where Miranda is?"

"She was in the morning room a few minutes ago."

She led me through the house and left me at the door of a sun-filled room. Miranda was at a window that overlooked the patio. She had daffodils in her hands and was arranging them in a bowl. The yellow flowers clashed with her somber clothes. The only color on her body was a scarlet bow at the neck of her black wool suit. Her small sharp breasts pressed angrily against the cloth.

"Good morning," she said. "I am expressing a wish, not making a statement."

"I understand that." The flesh around her eyes was swollen and faintly blue. "But I have some moderately good news for you."

"Moderately?" She raised her round chin, but her mouth remained doleful.

"We have some reason to think that your father is alive."

"Where is he?"

"I don't know."

"Then how do you know he's alive?"

"I didn't say I knew. I said I thought. I talked to one of his kidnappers."

She came at me headlong, clutching at my arm. "What did he say?"

"That your father is alive."

Her hand released my arm and took hold of her other hand. Her brown fingers interlocked and strained against each other. The daffodils fell to the floor with broken stems. "But you can't trust what they say? They'd naturally claim he's alive. What did they want? Did they phone you?"

"It was just one of them I talked to. Face to face."

"You saw him and let him go?"

"I didn't let him go. He's dead. His name is Alan Taggert."

"But that's impossible. I—" Her lower lip went slack and showed her lower row of teeth.

"Why is it impossible?" I said.

"He couldn't do it. He was decent. He was always honest with me—with us."

"Until the big chance came. Then he wanted money more than anything else. He was ready to murder to get it."

A question formed in her eyes. "You said Ralph was alive?"

"Taggert didn't murder your father. He tried to murder me."

"No," she said. "He wasn't like that. That woman twisted him. I knew she'd ruin him if he went with her."

"Did Taggert tell you about her?"

"Of course he told me. He told me everything."

"And you still loved him?"

"Did I say I loved him?" Her mouth was firm again and curved with pride.

"I understood you did."

"That stupid gawk? I used him for a while. He served the purpose."

"Stop it," I said violently. "You can't fool me, and you can't fool yourself. You'll tear yourself to pieces."

Yet her hands were motionless in each other, her tall body was still. Still as a tree bent out of line and held there by a continuous wind. The wind pushed her against me. Her feet trampled the daffodils. Her mouth closed over mine. Her body held me close from breast to knee, too long and not long enough.

"Thank you for killing him, Archer." Her voice was anguished and soft, the kind of voice a wound would have if it could speak.

I took her by the shoulders and held her off. "You're wrong. I didn't kill him."

"You said he was dead, that he tried to murder you."

"Albert Graves shot him."

"Albert?" Her giggle passed back and forth like a quick spark between laughter and hysteria. "Albert did that?"

"He's a dead shot—we used to do a lot of target-shooting together," I said. "If he wasn't, I wouldn't be here with you now."

"Do you like being here with me now?"

"It makes me a little sick. You're trying to swallow these things without going to pieces, and you can't get them down."

Her glance traveled down my body, and she grinned as much like a monkey as a pretty girl could. "Did it make you sick when I kissed you?"

"You could tell it didn't. But it's confusing to be in a room with five or six competing personalities."

"Sick-making, you mean," she said with her monkey grin.

"You'll be the sick one if you don't settle down. Find out what you feel about this business, and have a good cry, or you'll end up schizo."

"I always was a schizoid type," she said. "But why should I cry, *Herr Doktor?*"

"To see if you can."

"You don't take me seriously, do you, Archer?"

"I can't afford to put my hand in a cleft tree."

"My God," she said. "I'm sick-making, I'm schizo, I'm split wood. What do you really think of me?"

"I wouldn't know. I'd have a better idea if you'll tell me where you went last night."

"Last night? Nowhere."

"I understand you did a lot of driving in the red Packard convertible last night."

"I did, but I didn't go anywhere. I was just driving. I wanted to be by myself to make up my mind."

"About what?"

"About what I'm going to do. Do you know what I'm going to do, Archer?"

"No. Do you?"

"I want to see Albert," she said. "Where is he?"

"In the bathhouse, where it happened. Taggert's there, too."

"Take me to Albert."

We found him on the screened veranda sitting over the dead man. The sheriff and the District Attorney were looking at Taggert's face, which was still uncovered, and listening to Graves's story. All three stood up for Miranda.

She had to step over Taggert in order to reach Albert Graves. She did this without a downward glance at the uncovered face. She took one of Graves's hands between hers and raised it to her lips. It was his right hand she kissed, the one that had fired the gun.

"I'll marry you now," she said.

Whether Graves knew it or not, he'd had his reason for shooting Alan Taggert through the head.

chapter 26 *For half a minute nobody spoke.* The lovers stood together above the body. The others stood and watched them.

"We'd better get out of here, Miranda," Graves said finally. He glanced at the District Attorney. "If you'll excuse us? Mrs. Sampson will have to be told about this."

"Go ahead, Bert," Humphreys said.

While a man from his office took notes, and another photographed the body on the floor, Humphreys questioned me. His questions covered the ground quickly and thoroughly. I told him who Taggert was, how he died, and why he had to die. Sheriff Spanner listened restlessly, biting a cigar to shreds.

"There will have to be an inquest," Humphreys said. "You and Bert are in the clear, of course. Taggert had a deadly weapon in his hand and was obviously intending to use it. Unfortunately this shooting leaves us worse off than before. We have practically no leads."

"You're forgetting Betty Fraley."

"I'm not forgetting her. But we haven't caught her, and even if we do, we can't be certain that she knows where Sampson is. The problem hasn't changed, and we're no nearer to its solution than we were yesterday. The problem is to find Sampson."

"And the hundred thousand dollars," Spanner said.

Humphreys looked up impatiently. "The money is secondary, I think."

"Secondary, yes, but a hundred thousand in cash is always important." He tugged at his elastic lower lip. His gray eyes shifted to me. "If you're finished with Archer here, I want to have a talk with him."

"Take him," Humphreys said coldly. "I've got to get back to town." He took the body with him.

When we were alone the sheriff got up heavily and stood over me.

"Well?" I said. "What's the trouble, Sheriff?"

"Maybe you can tell me." He folded his thick arms across his chest.

"I've told you what I know."

"Maybe so. You didn't tell me everything you should of last night. I heard from your friend Colton this morning. He told me about the limousine this Lassiter was driving: it came from a car-rental in Pasadena, and you knew it." He raised his voice suddenly, as if he hoped to startle me into a confession. "You didn't tell me you saw it before, when the ransom note was delivered."

"I saw one like it. I didn't know it was the same car."

"But you guessed it was. You told Colton it was. You gave the information to an officer that couldn't use it because he's got no jurisdiction in this county. But you didn't tell me, did you? If you had, we could have taken him. We could have stopped the shooting and saved the money—"

"But not Sampson," I said.

"You're not the judge of that." His face was bursting at

the seams with angry blood. "You took things in your own hands and interfered with my duty. You withheld information. Right after Lassiter got shot, you disappeared. You were the only witness, and you disappeared. A hundred thousand dollars disappeared at the same time."

"I don't like the implication." I stood up. He was a big man, and our eyes were level.

"You don't like it. How do you think I like it? I'm not saying you took the money—that remains to be seen. I'm not saying you shot Lassiter. I'm saying you could have. I want your gun, and I want to know what you were doing when my deputy caught up with you down south. And I want to know what you were doing after that."

"I was looking for Sampson."

"You were looking for Sampson," he said, with heavy irony. "You expect me to take your word for that."

"You don't have to take my word. I'm not working for you."

He leaned toward me with his hands on his hips. "If I wanted to be ugly, I could put you away this minute."

My patience broke. "Don't look now," I said, "but you are ugly."

"Do you know who you're talking to?"

"A sheriff. A sheriff with a tough case on his hands, and no ideas. So you're looking for a goat."

The blood went out of his face, leaving it haggard with rage. "They'll hear about this in Sacramento," he stuttered. "When your license comes up—"

"I've heard that one before. I'm still in business, and I'll tell you why. I've got a clean record, and I don't push people around until they start to push me."

"So you're threatening me!" His right hand fumbled for the holster on his hip. "You're under arrest, Archer."

I sat down and crossed my legs. "Take it easy, Sheriff. Sit down and relax. We've got some things to talk over."

"I'll talk to you at the courthouse."

"No," I said. "Here. Unless you want to take me to the immigrant inspector."

"What's he got to do with it?" He wrinkled up his eyelids in an effort to look shrewd, and succeeded in looking puzzled. "You're not an alien?"

"I'm a native son," I said. "Is there an immigrant inspector in town?"

"Not in Santa Teresa. The nearest ones are at the federal office in Ventura. Why?"

"Do you do much work with them?"

"A fair amount. When I pick up an illegal alien I turn him over. You trying to kid me, Archer?"

"Sit down," I said again. "I didn't find what I was looking for last night, but I found something else. It should make you and the inspectors very happy. I'm offering it to you as a free gift, no strings."

He lowered his haunches into the canvas chair. His anger had passed off suddenly, and curiosity had taken its place. "What is it? It better be good."

I told him about the closed blue truck, the brown men at the Temple, Troy and Eddie and Claude. "Troy is the head of the gang, I'm pretty sure. The others work for him. They've been running an underground railway on a regular schedule between the Mexican border and the Bakersfield area. The southern end is probably at Calexico."

"Yeah," Spanner said. "That's an easy place to cross the

border. I took a trip down there with the border guard a couple of months ago. All they got to do is crawl through a wire fence from one road to the other."

"And Troy's truck would be waiting to pick them up. They used the Temple in the Clouds as a receiving station for illegal immigrants. God knows how many have passed through there. There were twelve or more last night."

"Are they still there?"

"They're in Bakersfield by now, but they shouldn't be hard to round up. If you get hold of Claude I'm pretty sure he'll talk."

"Jesus!" Spanner said. "If they brought over twelve a night, that's three hundred and sixty a month. Do you know how much they pay to get smuggled in?"

"No."

"A hundred bucks apiece. This Troy has been making big money."

"Dirty money," I said. "Trucking in a bunch of poor Indians, taking their savings away, and turning them loose to be migrant laborers."

He looked at me a little queerly. "They're breaking the law, too, don't forget. We don't prosecute, though, unless they got criminal records. We just ship them back to the border and let them go. But Troy and his gang are another matter. What they been doing is good for thirty years."

"That's fine," I said.

"You don't know where he hangs out in Los Angeles?"

"He runs a place called the Wild Piano, but he won't be showing there. I've told you what I know." With two exceptions: the man I had killed, and the blond woman who would still be waiting for Eddie.

"You seem to be on the level," the sheriff said slowly. "You can forget what I said about arrest. But if this turns out to be a song-and-dance you gave me, I'll remember it again."

I hadn't expected to be thanked, and I wasn't disappointed.

chapter **27**   I parked in the lane under the eucalyptus trees. The marks of the truck tires were still visible in the dust. Further down the lane a green A-model sedan, acned with rust, was backed against a fence post. On the registration card strapped to the steering gear I read the name, "Mrs. Marcella Finch."

The moonlight had been kind to the white cottage. It was ugly and mean and dilapidated in the noon sun, a dingy blot against the blue field of the sea. Nothing in sight lived or moved, except the sea itself and a few weak puffs of wind in the withered grass on the hillside. I felt for my gun butt. The dry dust muffled my footsteps.

The door creaked partly open when I knocked.

A woman's voice said dully: "Who's that?"

I stood aside and waited, in case she had a gun. She raised her voice. "Is somebody there?"

"Eddie," I whispered. Eddie had no further use for his name, but it was a hard thing to say.

"Eddie?" A hushed and wondering word.

I waited. Her sibilant feet crossed the floor. Before I could see her face in the dim interior, her right hand grasped the edge of the door. Under the peeling scarlet polish, her fingernails were dirty. I took hold of her hand.

"Eddie!" The face that looked around the door was blind with the sun and a desperate hopefulness. Then she blinked and saw I wasn't Eddie.

She had aged rapidly in twelve hours. She was puffed around the eyes, drawn at the mouth, drooping at the chin. Waiting for Eddie had drained away her life. A kind of galvanic fury took its place.

Her nails bit into my hand like parrot's claws. She squawked like a parrot: "Dirty liar!"

The name hit me hard, but not as hard as a bullet. I caught her other wrist and forced her back into the house, slamming the door with my heel. She tried to knee me, then to bite my neck. I pushed her down on the bed.

"I don't want to hurt you, Marcie."

From a round open mouth she screamed up into my face. The scream broke down in dry hiccuping. She flung herself sideways, burrowing under the covers. Her body moved in a rhythmic orgasm of grief. I stood above her and listened to the dry hiccuping.

Filtered through dirty windows, reflected from rain-stained walls and shabby furniture, the light in the room was gray. On top of an old battery radio beside the bed there were a handful of matches and a pack of cigarettes. She sat up after a while and lit a brown cigarette, dragging deep. Her bathrobe gaped open as if her slack breasts didn't matter any more.

The voice that came out with the smoke was contemptuous and flat. "I should stage a crying jag to give a copper his kicks."

"I'm no copper."

"You know my name. I been waiting all morning to hear

from the law." She looked at me with cold interest. "How low can you bastards get? You blow Eddie down when he ain't even heeled. Then you come and tell me you're Eddie at the door. For a minute you make me think the newscast was wrong or you bastards was bluffing again. Can you get any lower than that?"

"Not much," I said. "I thought you might answer the door with a gun."

"I got no gun. I never carried a gun, nor Eddie neither. You wouldn't be walking around if Eddie was heeled last night. Jumping for joy on his grave." The flat voice broke again. "Maybe I'll waltz on yours, copper."

"Be quiet for a minute. Listen to me."

"Gladly, gladly." The voice recaptured its tinny quality. "You'll be doing all the talking from now on. You can lock me up and throw away the key. You won't get nothing out of me."

"Douse the muggles, Marcie. I want you to talk some sense."

She laughed and blew smoke in my face. I took the half-burned cigarette from her fingers and ground it under my heel. The scarlet claws reached for my face. I stepped back, and she lapsed onto the bed.

"You must have been in on it, Marcie. You knew what Eddie was doing?"

"I deny everything. He had a job driving a truck. He trucked beans from the Imperial Valley." She stood up suddenly and threw off her bathrobe. "Take me down to headquarters and get it over. I'll deny everything formal."

"I don't belong to headquarters."

When she raised her arms to pull a dress over her head,

her body drew itself up, the breasts erect, the belly taut and white. The hair on her body was black.

"Like it?" she said. She pulled the dress down with a vicious gesture and fumbled with the buttons at the neck. Her streaked blond hair was down around her face.

"Sit down," I said. "We're not going anywhere. I came here to tell you a thing."

"Aren't you a copper?"

"You repeat yourself like Puddler. Listen to me. I want Sampson. I'm a private cop hired to find him. He's all I want —do you understand? If you can give him to me, I'll keep you in the clear."

"You're a dirty liar," she said. "I wouldn't trust a cop, private or any other kind. Anyway, I don't know where Sampson is."

I looked hard into her bird-brown eyes. They were shallow and meaningless. I couldn't tell from them if she was lying.

"You don't know where Sampson is—"

"I said I didn't."

"But you know who does."

She sat down on the bed. "I don't know a damn thing. I told you that."

"Eddie didn't do it by himself. He must have had a partner."

"He did it by himself. If he didn't—would you take me for a squealer? Do I go to work for the cops after what they done to Eddie?"

I sat down in the barrel chair and lit a cigarette. "I'll tell you a funny thing. I was there when Eddie was shot. There wasn't a cop within two miles, unless you count me."

"You killed him?" she said thinly.

"I did not. He stopped on a side road to pass the money to another car. It was a cream-colored convertible. It had a woman in it. She shot him. Where would that woman be now?"

Her eyes were glistening like wet brown pebbles. The red tip of her tongue moved across her upper lip and shifted to her lower lip. "Ever since she was on the white stuff," she said to herself. "They allus hate us vipers."

"Are you going to sit and take it, Marcie? Where is she?"

"I don't know who you're talking about."

"Betty Fraley," I said.

After a long silence she repeated: "I don't know who you're talking about."

I left her sitting on the bed and drove back to the Corner. I parked in the parking lot and lowered the sun screen over the windshield. She knew my face but not my car.

For half an hour the road from White Beach was empty. Then a cloud of dust appeared in the distance, towed by a green A-model sedan. Before the car turned south toward Los Angeles I caught a glimpse of a highly painted face, a swirl of gray fur, an aggressively tilted hat with a bright-blue feather. Clothes and cosmetics and half an hour alone had done a lot for Marcie.

Two or three other cars went by before I turned into the highway. The A model's top speed was under fifty, and it was easy to keep in sight. Driving slow on a hot day, down a highway I knew too well, the only trouble I had was staying awake. I narrowed the distance between us as we approached Los Angeles and the traffic increased.

The A model left the highway at Sunset Boulevard and went through Pacific Palisades without a pause. It labored

and trailed dark-blue oil smoke on the hills below the Santa
Monica Mountains. On the edge of Beverly Hills it left the
boulevard suddenly and disappeared.

I followed it up a winding road lined on both sides with
hedges. The A model was parked behind a laurel hedge in
the entrance to a gravel drive. In the instant of passing I saw
Marcie crossing the lawn toward a deep brick porch screened
with oleanders. She seemed to be thrust forward and hustled
along by a deadly energy.

chapter **28**   I turned at the next drive and
parked on the shoulder of the road, waiting for a signal to
break the suburban peace. The seconds piled up precariously
like a tower of poker chips.

I had the car door open and one foot in the road when the
Ford engine coughed. I drew in my leg and crouched down
behind the wheel. The Ford engine roared and went into
gear, then died away. A deeper sound took its place, and the
black Buick backed out of the drive. A man I didn't know
was at the wheel. The eyes in his fleshy face were like raisins
stuck in unbaked dough. Marcie was beside him in the front
seat. Gray hearselike curtains were drawn over the rear windows.

At the boulevard the Buick turned back toward the sea. I
followed as closely as I dared. Between Brentwood and Pacific Palisades it went off to the right, up a climbing road that
led into a canyon. I had the feeling that there wasn't much

mileage left in the Sampson case. We were coming into a narrow place for the end.

The road was cut in the western wall of the canyon. Below its unfenced edge was a tangle of underbrush. Above the road to my left a scattering of houses stood in roughly cleared patches. The houses were new and raw-looking. The opposite slope was scrub-oak wilderness.

From the top of a rise I caught a glimpse of the Buick climbing over the crest of the next hill. I accelerated on the downhill grade, crossed a narrow stone bridge that spanned a dry barranca, and climbed the hill after it. It was moving slowly down the other side, like a heavy black beetle feeling its way in unfamiliar territory. A rutted lane branched off to the right. The beetle paused and followed it.

I parked behind a tree, which half hid my car from below, and watched the Buick diminish down the lane. When it was no larger than an actual beetle, it stopped in front of a yellow matchbox house. A matchstick woman with a black head came out of the house. Two men and two women got out of the car and surrounded her. All five went into the house like a single insect body with many legs.

I left my car and climbed down through the underbrush to the dry river bed at the bottom of the canyon. It wound among boulders from which small lizards scampered as I came near. The gnarled trees along the bank hid me from the yellow house until I was directly behind it. It was an unpainted wooden shack with its rear end resting on short fieldstone columns.

Inside it a woman screamed, very loudly, again and again. The screams raked at my nerves, but I was grateful for them. They covered the noises I made climbing the bank and crawling under the house. The screaming died away after a while. I lay flat and listened to scrabbling movements on the floor above me. The silence under the house seemed to be crouched and waiting for another scream. I smelled new pine, damp earth, my own sour sweat.

A soft voice began to talk over my head. "You don't quite understand the circumstances. You seem to feel that our motive is pure sadism or simple revenge. Certainly if we were inclined to harbor vengeful motives, we might feel that your conduct had justified them."

"Tie a can to it, for Christ's sake!" said Mrs. Estabrook's voice. "This isn't getting us anywhere."

"I'll make my point if you don't mind. My point is, Betty, that you've acted very badly. Without consulting me, you went into business for yourself, a thing I seldom approve in my employees. To make matters worse, you made an incautious choice of enterprise and failed in it. The police are looking for you now, and for me and Fay and Luis as well. Furthermore, you chose a valuable associate of mine as the victim of your wretched little plot. And to cap the climax you showed yourself devoid, not only of esprit de corps, but of sisterly affection. You shot and killed your brother Eddie Lassiter."

"We know you swallowed the dictionary," Fay Estabrook said. "Get on with it, Troy."

"I didn't kill him." The whine of a hurt cat.

"You're a liar," yapped Marcie.

Troy raised his voice. "Be quiet, all of you. We're going to let bygones be bygones, Betty—"

"I'm going to kill her if you don't," Marcie said.

"Nonsense, Marcie. You'll do exactly as I say. We have a

chance to recoup, and we won't allow our more primitive passions to destroy it. Which brings us to the occasion of this pleasant little party, doesn't it, Betty? I don't know where the money is, but of course I am going to. And when I do, you'll have bought your absolution, so to speak."

"She ain't fit to live," Marcie said. "I swear I'll kill her if you don't."

Fay laughed contemptuously. "You haven't got the guts, dearie. You wouldn't have called us in if you had the guts to tackle her yourself."

"Hold your tongue, both of you." Troy lowered his voice to a gentle monotone again. "You know I can handle Marcie, don't you, Betty? I think you know by now I can handle even you. You might just as well come clean, I think. Otherwise you'll suffer rather terribly. You may never walk again, in fact. I think I can promise you that you never shall."

"I'm not talking," she said.

"But if you decide to co-operate," Troy went on smoothly, "to put the welfare of the group ahead of your selfish interest, I'm sure the group will be glad to help you in turn. We'll take you out of the country tonight, in fact. You know that Luis and I can do that for you."

"You wouldn't do it," she said. "I know you, Troy."

"More intimately by the moment, dear. Take off her other shoe, Luis."

Her body squirmed on the floor. I could hear its breathing. A dropped shoe rapped the floorboards. I calculated my chances of ending it there. But there were four of them, too many for one gun. And Betty Fraley had to come out alive.

Troy said: "We'll test the plantar reflex, I think it's called."

"I don't like this," Fay said.

"Neither do I, my dear. I quite abhor it. But Betty is being most dreadfully obdurate."

A moment of silence stretched out like membrane on the point of tearing. The screaming began again. When it ended I found that I had closed my teeth in the earth.

"Your plantar reaction is very fine," Troy said. "It's a pity that your tongue doesn't work so well."

"Will you let me go if I give it to you?"

"You have my word."

"Your word!" She sighed horribly.

"I do wish you'd take it, Betty. I don't enjoy hurting you, and you can't possibly enjoy being hurt."

"Let me up, then. Let me sit up."

"Of course, my dear."

"It's in a locker in the bus station in Buenavista. The key is in my bag."

As soon as I was out of sight of the house I began to run. When I reached my car the Buick was still standing at the end of the lane below me. I backed down the hill to the stone bridge and halfway up the grade on the other side. I waited for the Buick with one foot on the clutch and the other on the brake.

After a long while I heard its motor whining up the other side of the hill. I went into gear and moved ahead in low. Its chromium flashed in the sun at the top of the hill. I held the middle of the road and met it on the bridge. Brakes screeched above the bellow of the horn. The big car came to a stop five feet from my bumper. I was out of my seat before it stopped rolling.

The man called Luis glared at me over the wheel, his fat

face twisted and shiny with anger. I opened the door on his side and showed him my gun. Beside him Fay Estabrook cried out in fury.

"Out!" I said.

Luis put one foot down and reached for me. I moved back. "Be careful. Hands on your head."

He raised his hands and stepped into the road. An emerald ring flashed green on one of his fingers. His wide hips swayed under his cream gabardine suit.

"You too, Fay. This side."

She came out, teetering on her high heels.

"Now turn around."

They rotated cautiously, watching me over their shoulders. I clubbed the gun and swung it to the base of Luis's skull. He went down on his knees and collapsed softly on his face. Fay cowered away with her arms protecting her head. Her hat slipped forward dowdily over one eye. On the road her long shadow mocked her movements.

"Put him in the back seat," I said.

"You dirty little sneak!" she said. Then she said other things. The rouge stood out on her cheekbones.

"Hurry."

"I can't lift him."

"You have to." I took a step toward her.

She stooped awkwardly over the fallen man. He was inert, and heavy. With her hands in his armpits she raised the upper part of his body and dragged him to the car. I opened the door, and together we slung him into the back seat.

She stood up gasping for breath, the colors running in her face. The rustic stillness of the sun-filled canyon made a queer setting for what we were doing. I could see the two of us as if from a height, tiny foreshortened figures alone in the sun, with blood and money on our minds.

"Now give me the key."

"The key?" She overdid her puzzled frown, making her face a caricature. "What key?"

"The key to the locker, Fay. Hurry."

"I haven't got any key." But her gaze had flickered almost imperceptibly toward the front seat of the Buick.

There was a black suede purse on the seat. The key was in it. I transferred it to my wallet.

"Get in," I said. "No, on the driver's side. You're going to do the driving."

She did as I said, and I got in behind her. Luis was slumped in the far corner of the back seat. His eyes were partly open, but the pupils were turned up out of sight. His face looked more than ever like dough.

"I can't get past your car," Fay said petulantly.

"You're backing up the hill."

She went into reverse gear with a jerk.

"Not so fast," I said. "If we have an accident you won't survive it."

She cursed me, but she also slowed down. She backed cautiously up the hill and down the other side. At the entrance to the lane I told her to turn and drive down to the cottage.

"Slow and careful, Fay. No leaning on the horn. You wouldn't be any good without a spinal column, and Geminis have no heart."

I touched the back of her neck with the muzzle of my gun. She winced, and the car leaped forward. I rested my weight on Luis and lowered the rear window on the right side. The lane opened out in a small level clearing in front of the cottage.

"Turn left," I said, "and stop in front of the door. Then set the emergency."

The door of the cottage began to open inward. I ducked my head. When I raised it again, Troy was in the doorway, with his right hand, knuckles out, resting on the edge of the frame. I sighted and fired. At twenty feet I could see the mark the bullet made, like a fat red insect alighting, between the first and second knuckles of his right hand.

Before his left hand could move across his body for his gun he was immobile for an instant. Long enough for me to reach him and use the gun butt again. He sat down on the doorstep, with his silver head hanging between his knees.

The motor of the Buick roared behind me. I went after Fay, caught the car before she could turn it, and pulled her out by the shoulders. She tried to spit at me and slobbered on her chin.

"We'll go inside," I said. "You first."

She walked almost drunkenly, stumbling on her heels. Troy had rolled out of the doorway and was curled on the shallow porch, perfectly still. We stepped over him.

The odor of burned flesh was still in the room. Betty Fraley was on the floor with Marcie at her throat, worrying her like a terrier. I pulled Marcie off. She hissed at me and drummed her heels on the floor, but she didn't try to get up. I motioned to Fay with the gun to stand in the corner beside her.

Betty Fraley sat up, the breath whistling in her throat. Across one side of her face, from hairline to jawbone, four

parallel scratches dripped blood. The other side of her face
was yellowish white.

"You're a pretty picture," I said.

"Who are you?" Her voice was a flat caw. Her eyes were
fixed.

"It doesn't matter. Let's get out of here before I have to
kill these people."

"That would be pleasant work," she said. She tried to
stand up and fell forward on hands and knees. "I can't walk."

I lifted her. Her body was light and hard as a dry stick. Her
head hung loosely across my arm. I had the feeling that I was
holding an evil child. Marcie and Fay were watching me from
the corner. It seemed to me then that evil was a female quality, a poison that women secreted and transmitted to men
like disease.

I carried Betty out to the car and sat her down in the front
seat. I opened the back door, laid Luis out on the ground.
There were suds on his thick blue lips, blown in and out by
his shallow breathing.

"Thank you," her tiny caw said, as I climbed behind the
wheel. "You saved my life, if that's worth anything."

"It isn't worth much, but you're going to pay me for it.
The price is a hundred thousand—and Ralph Sampson."

chapter 29   I parked the Buick in the road at
the entrance to the bridge and kept the ignition key. As I
lifted Betty Fraley out of the seat her right arm slipped

around my shoulders. I could feel her small fingers on the nape of my neck.

"You're very strong," she said. "You're Archer, aren't you?" She looked up at me with a sly and feline innocence. She didn't know about the blood on her face.

"It's time you remembered me. Take your hand off me, or I'll drop you."

She lowered her eyelids. When I started to back my car she cried out suddenly:

"What about them?"

"We don't have room for them."

"You're going to let them go?"

"What do you want me to hold them for? Mayhem?" I found a wide place in the road and turned the car toward Sunset Boulevard.

Her fingers pinched my arm. "We've got to go back."

"I told you to keep your hands off me. I don't like what you did to Eddie any more than they do."

"But they've got something of mine!"

"No," I said. "I have it, and it isn't yours any more."

"The key?"

"The key."

She slumped down in the seat as if her spine had melted. "You can't let them go," she said sullenly. "After what they did to me. You let Troy run loose, and he'll get you for to-day."

"I don't think so," I said. "Forget about them and start worrying about yourself."

"I haven't got a future to worry about. Have I?"

"I want to see Sampson first. Then I'll decide."

"I'll take you to him."

"Where is he?"

"Not very far from home. He's in a place on the beach about forty miles from Santa Teresa."

"This is straight?"

"The straight stuff, Archer. But you won't let me go. You won't take money, will you?"

"Not from you."

"Why should you?" she said nastily. "You've got my hundred grand."

"I'm working for the Sampsons. They'll get it back."

"They don't need the money. Why don't you get smart, Archer? There's another person in this with me. This other person had nothing to do with Eddie. Why don't you keep the money and split it with this other person?"

"Who is he?"

"I didn't say it was a man." Her voice had recovered from the pressure of Marcie's fingers, and she modulated it girlishly.

"You couldn't work with a woman. Who's the man?" She didn't know that Taggert was dead, and it wasn't the time to tell her.

"Forget it. I thought for a minute maybe I could trust you. I must be going soft in the head."

"Maybe you are. You haven't told me where Sampson is. The longer it takes you to tell me, the less I'll feel like doing anything for you."

"He's in a place on the beach about ten miles north of Buenavista. It used to be the dressing-room of a beach club that folded during the war."

"And he's alive?"

"He was yesterday. The first day he was sick from the chloroform, but he's all right now."

"He was yesterday, you mean. Is he tied up?"

"I haven't seen him. Eddie was the one."

"I suppose you left him there to starve to death."

"I couldn't go there. He knew me by sight. Eddie was the one he didn't know."

"And Eddie died by an act of God."

"No, I killed him." She said it almost smugly. "You'll never be able to prove it, though. I wasn't thinking of Sampson when I shot Eddie."

"You were thinking of money, weren't you? A two-way cut instead of a three-way cut."

"I admit it was partly that, but only partly. Eddie pushed me around all the time I was a kid. When I finally got on my feet and was heading places, he sang me into the pen. I was using the stuff, but he was selling it. He helped the feds to hang conspiracy on me, and got off with a light sentence himself. He didn't know I knew that, but I promised myself to get him. I got him when he thought he was riding high. Maybe he wasn't so surprised. He told Marcie where to find me if anything went wrong."

"It always does," I said. "Kidnappings don't come off. Especially when the kidnappers start murdering each other."

I turned onto the boulevard and stopped at the first gas station I came to. She watched me remove the ignition key.

"What are you going to do?"

"Phone help for Sampson. He may be dying, and it's going to take us an hour and a half to get there. Has the place got a name?"

"It used to be the Sunland Beach Club. It's a long green building. You can see it from the highway, out near the end of a little point."

For the first time I was sure she was telling the truth. I called Santa Teresa from the station's pay telephone while the attendant filled the tank of my car. I could watch Betty Fraley through the window.

Felix answered the phone. "This is the Sampson residence."

"Archer speaking. Is Mr. Graves there?"

"Yes, sir. I will call him."

Graves came to the phone. "Where the hell are you?"

"Los Angeles. Sampson is alive, or at least he was yesterday. He's locked up in the dressing-room of a beach club called the Sunland. Know it?"

"I used to. It's been out of business for years. I know where it is, north of Buenavista on the highway."

"See how fast you can get there with first aid and food. And you better bring a doctor and the sheriff."

"Is he in bad shape?"

"I don't know. He's been alone since yesterday. I'll be there as soon as I can."

I hung up on Graves and called Peter Colton. He was still on duty.

"I've got something for you," I said. "Partly for you and partly for the Department of Justice."

"Another migraine headache, no doubt." He didn't sound glad to hear from me. "This Sampson case is the mess of the century."

"It was. I'm closing it today."

His voice dropped a full octave. "Say again, please."

"I know where Sampson is, and I've got the last of the kidnap gang with me now."

"Don't be coy, for Christ's sake! Spill it. Where is he?"

"Out of your territory, in Santa Teresa County. The Santa Teresa sheriff is on his way to him now."

"So you called up to brag, you poor narcissistic bastard. I thought you had something for me and the Department of Justice."

"I have, but not the kidnapping. Sampson wasn't carried across the state line, so the F.B.I. is out. The case has by-products, though. There's a canyon feeding into Sunset between Brentwood and the Palisades. The road that leads into it is Hopkins Lane. About five miles in, there's a black Buick sedan in the road, past that a lane leading down to an unpainted pine cottage. There are four people in the cottage. One of them is Troy. Whether it knows it or not, the Department of Justice wants them."

"What for?"

"Smuggling illegal immigrants. I'm in a hurry. Have I said enough?"

"For the present," he said. "Hopkins Lane."

Betty Fraley looked at me blankly when I went back to the car. Meaning returned to her eyes like a snake coming out of its hole. "Little man, what now?" she said.

"I did you a favor. I called the police to pick up Troy and the others."

"And me?"

"I'm saving you." I headed down Sunset towards U.S. 101.

"I'll turn state's evidence against him," she said.

"You don't have to. I can pin it on him myself."

"The smuggling rap?"

"Right. Troy disappointed me. Trucking in Mexicans is a pretty low-grade racket for a gentleman crook. He should be selling Hollywood Bowl to visiting firemen."

"It paid him well. He made it pay off double. He took the poor creeps' money for the ride, then turned them over to the ranches at so much a head. The Mexicans didn't know it, but they were being used as strikebreakers. That way Troy got protection from some of the local cops. Luis greased the Mexican federals at the other end."

"Was Sampson buying strikebreakers from Troy?"

"He was, but you'd never prove it. Sampson was very careful to keep himself in the clear."

"He wasn't careful enough," I said. She was silent after that.

As I turned north on the highway I noticed that her face was ugly with pain. "There's a pint of whisky in the glove compartment. You can use it to clean your burns and the scratches on your face. Or you can drink it."

She followed both suggestions and offered me the open bottle.

"Not for me."

"Because I drank from it first? All my diseases are mental."

"Put it away."

"You don't like me, do you?"

"Poison isn't my drink. Not that you don't have your points. You seem to have some brains, on a low level."

"Thanks for nothing, my intellectual friend."

"And you've been around."

"I'm not a virgin, if you're talking about that. I haven't been since I was eleven. Eddie saw a chance to turn a dollar. But I never did my living below the belt. The music saved me from that."

"It's too bad it didn't save you from this."

"I took my chance. It didn't work out. What makes you think I care one way or the other?"

"You care about this other person. You want him to have the money, no matter what happens to you."

"I told you to forget that." After a pause she said: "You could let me go and keep the money yourself. You'll never have another crack at a hundred grand."

"Neither will you, Betty. Neither will Alan Taggert."

She uttered a groan of surprise and shock. When she recovered her voice she said in a hostile tone: "You've been kidding me. What do you know about Taggert?"

"What he told me."

"I don't believe you. He never told you a thing." She corrected herself. "He doesn't know anything to tell."

"He did."

"Did something happen to him?"

"Death happened to him. He's got a hole in the head like Eddie."

She started to say something, but the words were broken up by a rush of crying, a high drawn-out whimper giving place to steady dry sobs. After a long time she whispered:

"Why didn't you tell me he was dead?"

"You didn't ask me. Were you crazy about him?"

"Yes," she said. "We were crazy about each other."

"If you were so crazy about him, why did you drag him into a thing like this?"

"I didn't drag him in. He wanted to do it. We were going to go away together."

"And live happily ever after."

"Keep your cheap cracks to yourself."

"I won't buy love's young dream from you, Betty. He was a boy, and you're an old woman, as experience goes. I think you sucked him in. You needed a finger man, and he looked easy."

"That's not the way it was." Her voice was surprisingly gentle. "We've been together for half a year. He came into the Piano with Sampson the week after I opened. I fell, and it was the same with him. But neither of us had anything. We had to have money to make a clean break."

"And Sampson was the obvious source. Kidnapping was the obvious method."

"You don't have to waste your sympathy on Sampson. But we had other ideas at first. Alan was going to marry the girl, Sampson's daughter, and get Sampson to buy him off. Sampson spoilt that himself. He lent Alan his bungalow at the Valerio one night. In the middle of the night we caught Sampson behind the curtains in the bedroom peeping at us. After that Sampson told the girl that if she married Alan he'd cut her off. He was going to fire Alan too, only we knew too much about him."

"Why didn't you blackmail him? That would be more your line."

"We thought of that, but he was too big for us to handle and he has the best lawyers in the state. We knew plenty about him, but he would be hard to pin down. This Temple in the Clouds, for example. How could we prove that Sampson knew what Troy and Claude and Fay were using it for?"

"If you know so much about Sampson," I said, "what makes him tick?"

"That's a hard one. I used to think maybe he had some faggot blood, but I don't know. He's getting old, and I guess he felt washed up. He was looking for anything that would make him feel like a man again: astrology or funny kinds of sex, anything at all. The only thing he cares about is his daughter. I think he caught on that she was stuck on Alan, and never forgave Alan."

"Taggert should have stuck to her," I said.

"You think so?" Her voice cracked. It was humble and small when she spoke again. "I didn't do him any good. I know that, you don't have to tell me. I couldn't help myself, and neither could he. How did he die, Archer?"

"He got into a tight corner and tried to push out with a gun. Somebody else shot first. A man called Graves."

"I'd like to meet that man. You said before that Alan talked. He didn't do that?"

"Not about you."

"I'm glad of that," she said. "Where is he now?"

"In the morgue in Santa Teresa."

"I wish I could see him—once more."

The words came softly out of a dark dream. In the silence that followed, the dream spread beyond her mind and cast a shadow as long as the shadows thrown by the setting sun.

chapter **30**   When I slowed down for Buena-vista, twilight was softening the ugliness of the buildings and the lights were going on along the main street. I noticed the neon greyhound at the bus station but didn't stop. A few miles beyond the town the highway converged with the shoreline again, winding along the bluffs above the uninhabited beaches. The last gray shreds of daylight clung to the surface of the sea and were slowly absorbed.

"This is it," Betty Fraley said. She had been so still I'd almost forgotten she was in the seat beside me.

I stopped on the asphalt shoulder of the highway, just short of a crossroads. On the ocean side the road slanted down to the beach. A weather-faded sign at the corner advertised a desirable beach development, but there were no houses in sight. I could see the old beach club, though, a mass of buildings two hundred yards below the highway, long and low and neutral-colored against the glimmering whiteness of the surf.

"You can't drive down," she said. "The road's washed out at the bottom."

"I thought you hadn't been down there."

"Not since last week. I looked it over with Eddie when he found it. Sampson's in one of the little rooms on the men's side of the dressing-rooms."

"He better be."

I took the ignition key and left her in the car. As I went down, the road narrowed to a humped clay pathway with deeply eroded ditches on both sides. The wooden platform in front of the first building was warped, and I could feel the clumps of grass growing up through the cracks under my feet. The windows were high under the eaves, and dark.

I turned my flashlight on the twin doors in the middle, and saw the stencilled signs: "Gentlemen" on one, "Ladies" on the other. The one on the right, for "Gentlemen," was hanging partly open. I pulled it wide, but not very hopefully. The place seemed empty and dead. Except for the restless water, there was no sign of life in it or around it.

No sign of Sampson, and no sign of Graves. I looked at my watch, which said a quarter to seven. It was well over an hour since I'd called Graves. He'd had plenty of time to drive the forty-five miles from Cabrillo Canyon. I wondered what had happened to him and the sheriff.

I shot my flashlight beam across the floor, which was covered with blown sand and the detritus of years. Opposite me was a row of closed doors in a plywood partition. I took a step toward the row of doors. The movement behind me was so lizard-quick I had no time to turn. "Ambush" was the last word that flashed across my consciousness before it faded out.

"Sucker" was the first word when consciousness returned. The cyclops eye of an electric lantern stared down at me like the ghastly eye of conscience. My impulse was to get up and fight. The deep voice of Albert Graves inhibited the impulse:

"What happened to you?"

"Turn the lantern away." Its light went through my eye sockets like swords and out at the back of my skull.

He set the lantern down and kneeled beside me. "Can you get up, Lew?"

"I can get up." But I stayed where I was on the floor. "You're late."

"I had some trouble finding the place in the dark."

"Where's the sheriff? Couldn't you find him either?"

"He was out on a case, committing a paranoiac to the county hospital. I left word for him to follow me down and bring a doctor. I didn't want to waste time."

"It looks to me as if you've wasted a lot of time."

"I thought I knew the place, but I must have missed it. I drove on nearly to Buenavista before I realized it. Then when I came back I couldn't find it."

"Didn't you see my car?"

"Where?"

I sat up. A swaying sickness moved back and forth like a pendulum in my head. "At the corner just above here."

"That's where I parked. I didn't see your car."

I felt for my car keys. They were in my pocket. "You're sure? They didn't take my car keys."

"Your car isn't there, Lew. Who are they?"

"Betty Fraley and whoever sapped me. There must have been a fourth member of the gang guarding Sampson." I told him how I had come there.

"It wasn't smart to leave her in the car," he said.

"Three sappings in two days are making Jack a dull boy."

I got to my feet and found that my legs were weak. He offered his shoulder for me to lean on. I leaned against the wall.

He raised the lantern. "Let me look at your head." The broad planes of his face in the moving light were furrowed by anxiety. He looked heavy and old.

"Later," I said.

I picked up my flashlight and crossed to the row of doors. Sampson was waiting behind the second one, a fat old man slumped on a bench against the rear wall of the cubicle. His head was wedged upright in the corner. His open eyes were suffused with blood.

Graves crowded in behind me and said: "God!"

I handed him the flashlight and bent over Sampson. His

hands and ankles were bound together with quarter-inch
rope, one end of which was strung through a staple in the
wall. The other end of the rope was sunk in Sampson's neck
and tied under his left ear in a hard knot. I reached behind
the body for one of the bound wrists. It wasn't cold, but the
pulse was gone. The pupils of the red eyeballs were asymmet-
ric. There was something pathetic about the bright plaid
socks, yellow and red and green, on the thick dead ankles.

Graves's breath came out. "Is he dead?"

"Yes." I felt a terrific letdown, which was followed by
inertia. "He must have been alive when I got here. How long
was I out?"

"It's a quarter after seven now."

"I got here about a quarter to. They've had a half-hour's
start. We've got to move."

"And leave Sampson here?"

"Yes. The police will want him this way."

We left him in the dark. I drew on my last reserve to get
up the hill. My car was gone. Graves's Studebaker was parked
at the other side of the intersection.

"Which way?" he said, as he climbed behind the wheel.

"Buenavista. We'll go to the highway patrol."

I looked in my wallet, expecting the locker key to be gone.
But it was there, tucked in the card compartment. Whoever
sapped me hadn't had a chance to compare notes with Betty
Fraley. Or they decided to make their getaway and let the
money go. Somehow that didn't seem likely.

I said to Graves, as we passed the town limits: "Drop me
at the bus station."

"Why?"

I told him why, and added: "If the money's there, they

may be back for it. If it isn't, it probably means they came this way and broke open the locker. You go to the highway patrol and pick me up later."

He let me out at the red curb in front of the bus station. I stood outside the glass door and looked into the big square waiting-room. Three or four men in overalls were slouched on the scarred benches reading newspapers. A few old men, ancient-looking in the fluorescent lights, were leaning against the poster-papered walls and talking among themselves. A Mexican family in one corner, father and mother and several children, formed a solid unit like a six-man football team. The ticket booth under the clock at the back of the room was occupied by a pimply youth in a flowered Hawaiian shirt. There was a doughnut counter to the left, a fat blond woman in uniform behind it. The bank of green metal lockers was against the wall to the right.

None of the people in the room showed the tension I was looking for. They were waiting for ordinary things: supper, a bus, Saturday night, a pension check, or a natural death in bed.

I pushed the glass door open and crossed the butt-strewn floor to the lockers. The number I wanted was stamped on the key: twenty-eight. As I pushed the key into the lock I glanced around the room. The doughnut woman's boiled blue eyes were watching me incuriously. Nobody else seemed interested.

There was a red canvas beach bag in the locker. When I pulled it out I could hear the rattling paper inside. I sat down on the nearest empty bench and opened the bag. The brown paper package it contained was torn open at one end. I felt the edges of the stiff new bills with my fingers.

I tucked the bag under my arm, went to the doughnut counter, and ordered coffee.

"Did you know you got blood on your shirt?" the blond woman said.

"I know it. I wear it that way."

She looked me over as if she doubted my ability to pay. I restrained the impulse I had to give her a hundred-dollar bill, and slapped a dime on the counter. She gave me coffee in a thick white cup.

I watched the door as I drank it, holding the cup in my left hand, with my right hand ready to take out my gun. The electric clock above the ticket booth took little bites of time. A bus arrived and departed, shuffling the occupants of the room. The clock chewed very slowly, masticating each minute sixty times. By ten to eight it was too late to hope for them. They had by-passed the money or gone the other way.

Graves appeared in the doorway gesticulating violently. I set down my cup and followed him out. His car was double-parked across the street.

"They just wrecked your car," he told me, on the sidewalk. "About fifteen miles north of here."

"Did they get away?"

"Apparently one of them did. The Fraley woman's dead."

"What happened to the other?"

"The H.P. don't know yet. All they had was the first radio report."

We covered the fifteen miles in less than fifteen minutes. The place was marked by a line of standing cars, a crowd of human figures like animated black cut-outs in the headlights. Graves pulled up short of a policeman who was trying to wave us on with a red-beamed flashlight.

Standing on the running board, I could see beyond the line of cars to the edge of the swathe of light. My car was there, its nose crumpled into the bank. I took off at a run and elbowed my way through the crowd around the wreck.

A highway patrolman with a seamed brown face put his hand on my arm. I shook it off. "This is my car."

His eyes narrowed, and the sun wrinkles fanned back to his ears. "You sure? What's your name?"

"Archer."

"It's yours all right. That's who she's registered to." He called out to a young patrolman who was standing uneasily by his motorcycle: "Come here, Ollie! It's this guy's car."

The crowd began to re-form, focusing on me. When they broke their tight circle around the smashed car, I could see the blanket-covered figure on the ground beside it. I pushed between a pair of women whose eyes were drinking it in, and lifted one end of the blanket. The object underneath wasn't recognizably human, but I knew it by its clothes.

Two of them in an hour were too much for me, and my stomach revolted. Empty of everything but the coffee I had drunk, it brought up bitterness. The two patrolmen waited until I was able to talk.

"This woman steal your car?" the older one said.

"Yes. Her name is Betty Fraley."

"The office said they had a bulletin on her—"

"That's right. But what happened to the other one?"

"What other one?"

"There was a man with her."

"Not when she wrecked the car," the young patrolman said.

"You can't be sure."

"I am sure, though. I saw it happen. I was responsible in a way."

"Naw, naw, Ollie." The older man put his hand on Ollie's shoulder. "You did exactly the right thing. Nobody's going to blame you."

"Anyway," Ollie blurted, "I'm glad the car was hot."

That irritated me. The convertible was insured, but it would be hard to replace. Besides, I had a feeling for it, the kind of feeling a rider has for his horse.

"What did happen?" I asked him sharply.

"I was tooling along about fifty a few miles south of here, heading north. This dame in the convertible passed me as if I was standing still, and I gave chase. I was traveling around ninety before I started to pull up on her. Even when I was abreast of her, she went right on gunning down the road. She didn't pay any attention when I signaled to pull over, so I cut in ahead. She swerved and tried to pass me on the right and lost control of the car. It skidded a couple of hundred feet and piled up in the bank. When I pulled her out of it she was dead."

His face was wet when he finished. The older man shook him gently by the shoulder. "Don't let it worry you, kid. You got to enforce the law."

"You're absolutely sure," I asked, "there was nobody else in the car?"

"Unless they went up in smoke— It's a funny thing," he added in a high, nervous voice, "there was no fire, but the soles of her feet were blistered. And I couldn't find her shoes. She was in her bare feet."

"That is funny," I said. "Extremely funny."

Albert Graves had forced his way through the crowd. "They must have had another car."

"Then why would she bother with mine?" I reached inside the wreck, under the warped and bloody dashboard, and felt the ignition wires. The terminals had been reconnected with the copper wire I had left there in the morning. "She had to rewire my ignition to start the engine."

"That's more like a man's work, isn't it?"

"Not necessarily. She could have picked it up from her brother. Every car thief knows the trick."

"Maybe they decided to split up for the getaway."

"Maybe, but I don't see it. She was smart enough to know my car would identify her."

"I got to fill out a report," the older patrolman said. "Can you spare a few minutes?"

While I was answering the last of the questions, Sheriff Spanner arrived in a radio car driven by a deputy. The two of them got out and trotted toward us. Spanner's heavy chest bounced almost like a woman's as he ran.

"What's been happening?" He looked from me to Graves with moist, suspicious eyes.

I let Graves tell him. When he had heard what had happened to Sampson and Betty Fraley, Spanner turned back to me.

"You see what's come of your meddling, Archer. I warned you to work under my supervision."

I wasn't in the mood to take it quietly. "Supervision, hell! If you'd got to Sampson soon enough, he might be alive now."

"You knew where he was, and you didn't tell me about it," he yammered. "You're going to suffer for that, Archer."

"Yeah, I know. When my license comes up for renewal. You said that before. But what are you going to tell Sacramento about your own incompetence? You're out at the county hospital committing a loony when the case is breaking wide open."

"I haven't been out at the hospital since yesterday," he said. "What are you talking about?"

"Didn't you get my message about Sampson? A couple of hours ago?"

"There was no message. You can't cover yourself that way."

I looked at Graves. His eyes avoided mine. I held my tongue.

An ambulance with its siren whooping came down the highway from the direction of Santa Teresa.

"They take their time," I said to the patrolman.

"They knew she was dead. No hurry."

"Where will they take her?"

"The morgue in Santa Teresa, unless she's claimed."

"She won't be. It's a good place for her."

Alan Taggert and Eddie, her lover and her brother, were there already.

chapter **31**   Graves drove very slowly, as if the sight of the wreck had had an effect on him. It took us nearly an hour to get back to Santa Teresa. I spent it thinking—about Albert Graves and then about Miranda. My thoughts were poor company.

He looked at me curiously as we entered the city. "I wouldn't give up hope, Lew. The police have a good chance to catch him."

"Who do you mean?"

"The murderer, of course. The other man."

"I'm not sure there was another man."

His hands tightened on the wheel. I could see the knuckles stand out. "But somebody killed Sampson."

"Yes," I said. "Somebody did."

I watched his eyes as they turned slowly to meet mine. He looked at me coldly for a long moment.

"Watch your driving, Graves. Watch everything."

He turned his face to the road again, but not before I had caught its look of shame.

Where the highway crossed the main street of Santa Teresa, he stopped for a red light. "Where do we go from here?"

"Where do you want to go?"

"It doesn't matter to me."

"We'll go to the Sampson place," I said. "I want to talk to Mrs. Sampson."

"Do you have to do it now?"

"I'm working for her. I owe her a report."

The light changed. Nothing more was said until we turned up the drive to the Sampson house. Its dark mass was pierced by a few lights.

"I don't want to see Miranda if it can be helped," he said. "We were married this afternoon."

"Didn't you jump the gun a little?"

"What do you mean by that? I've been carrying the license for months."

"You might have waited until her father was home. Or decently laid away."

"She wanted it done today," he said. "We were married in the courthouse."

"You'll probably be spending your wedding night there. The jail's in the same building, isn't it?"

He didn't answer. When he stopped the car by the garages, I leaned forward to look into his face. He had swallowed the shame. Nothing was left but a gambler's resignation.

"It's an ironic thing," he said. "This is our wedding night, the night that I've been waiting for for years. And now I don't want to see her."

"Do you expect me to leave you out here by yourself?"

"Why not?"

"I can't trust you. You were the one man I thought I could trust—" I couldn't find the words to end the sentence.

"You can trust me, Lew."

"We'll make it Mr. Archer from now on."

"Mr. Archer, then. I've got a gun in my pocket. But I'm not going to use it. I've had enough of violence. Do you understand that? I'm sick of it."

"You should be sick," I said, "with two murders on your stomach. You've had your fill of violence for a while."

"Why did you say two murders, Lew?"

"Mr. Archer," I said.

"You don't have to take a high moral tone. I didn't plan it this way."

"Not many do. You shot Taggert on the spur of the moment, and you've improvised ever since. Toward the end you've been getting pretty careless. You might have known I'd find out you didn't call the sheriff tonight."

"You can't prove you told me to."

"I don't have to. But it was enough to let me know what you were up to. You wanted to be alone with Sampson in that shack for a little while. You had to finish the job that Taggert's partners had failed to do for you."

"Do you seriously think I had anything to do with the kidnapping?"

"I know damn well you didn't. But the kidnapping has something to do with you. It made a murderer out of you by giving you a reason to kill Taggert."

"I shot Taggert in good faith," he said. "I admit I wasn't sorry to have him out of the way. Miranda liked him too well. But the reason I shot him was to save you."

"I don't believe you." I sat there in cold anger. The stars clung like snow crystals in the black sky, pouring cold down on my head.

"I didn't plan it," he said. "I had no time to plan it. Taggert was going to shoot you, and I shot him instead. It was as simple as that."

"Killing is never simple, not when it's done by a man with your brains. You're a dead shot, Graves. You didn't have to kill him."

He answered me harshly. "Taggert deserved to die. He got what was coming to him."

"But not at the right time. I've been wondering how much you heard of what he said to me. You must have heard enough to know he was one of the kidnappers. Probably enough to be pretty sure that if Taggert died, his partners would kill Sampson."

"I heard very little. I saw he was going to shoot you, and

I shot him instead." The iron returned to his voice. "Evidently I made a mistake."

"You made several mistakes. The first was killing Taggert—that's what started it all, isn't it? It wasn't really Taggert you wanted dead. It was Sampson himself. You never wanted Sampson to come home alive, and you thought that by killing Taggert you'd arranged that. But Taggert had only one surviving partner, and she was hiding out. She didn't even know Taggert was dead until I told her, and she had no chance to kill Sampson, though she probably would have if she'd had the chance. So you had to murder Sampson for yourself."

Shame, and what looked like uncertainty, pulled at his face again. He shook them off. "I'm a realist, Archer. So are you. Sampson's no loss to anybody."

His voice had changed, become suddenly shallow and flat. The whole man was shifting and fencing, trying out attitudes, looking for one that would sustain him.

"You're taking murder more lightly than you used to," I said. "You've sent men to the gas chamber for murder. Has it occurred to you that that's where you're probably headed?"

He managed to smile. The smile made deep and ugly lines around his mouth and between his eyes. "You have no proof against me. Not a scrap."

"I have moral certainty and your own implicit confession—"

"But no record of it. You haven't even enough to bring me to trial."

"It isn't my job to do that. You know where you stand,

better than I do. I don't know why you had to murder Sampson."

He was silent for some time. When he spoke, his voice had changed again. It was candid and somehow young, the voice of the man I had known in bull sessions years ago. "It's strange that you should say that I had to, Lew. That was how I felt. I had to do it. I hadn't made up my mind until I found Sampson there by himself in the dressing-room. I didn't even speak to him. I saw what could be done, and once I'd seen it, I had to do it whether I liked it or not."

"I think you liked it."

"Yes," he said. "I liked killing him. Now I can't bear to think of it."

"Aren't you being a little easy on yourself? I'm no analyst, but I know you had other motives. More obvious and not so interesting. You got married this afternoon to a girl who was potentially very rich. If her father was dead she was actually very rich. Don't tell me you're not aware that you and your bride have been worth five million dollars for the last couple of hours."

"I know it well enough," he said. "But it's not five million. Mrs. Sampson gets half."

"I forgot about her. Why didn't you kill her too?"

"You're bearing down pretty hard."

"You bore down harder on Sampson, for a paltry million and a quarter. Half of one half of his money. Weren't you being a piker, Graves? Or were you planning to murder Mrs. Sampson and Miranda later on?"

"You know that isn't true," he said tonelessly. "What do you think I am?"

"I haven't made up my mind. You're a man who married

a girl and killed her father the same day to convert her into an heiress. What was the matter, Graves? Didn't you want her without a million-dollar dowry? I thought you were in love with her."

"Lay off." His voice was tormented. "Leave Miranda out of it."

"I can't. If it wasn't for Miranda, we might have something more to talk about."

"No," he said. "There's nothing more to talk about."

I left him sitting in the car, smiling his stony gambler's smile. My back was to him as I crossed the gravel drive to the house, and he had a gun in his pocket, but I didn't look back. I believed him when he said he was sick of violence.

The lights were on in the kitchen, but nobody answered my knock. I went through the house to the elevator. Mrs. Kromberg was in the upstairs hall when I stepped out.

"Where are you going?"

"I have to see Mrs. Sampson."

"You can't. She's been awful nervous today. She took three grains of nembutal about an hour ago."

"This is important."

"How important?"

"The thing she's been waiting to hear."

Comprehension flickered in her eyes, but she was too good a servant to question me. "I'll see if she's asleep." She went to the closed door of Mrs. Sampson's room and opened it quietly.

A frightened whisper came from inside the room. "Who's that?"

"Kromberg. Mr. Archer says he has to see you. He says it's very important."

"Very well," the whisper said. A light was switched on. Mrs. Kromberg stood back to let me enter.

Mrs. Sampson leaned on her elbows, blinking in the light. Her brown face was drugged and sodden with sleep or the hope of sleep. The round dark tips of her breasts stared through the silk pajamas like dull eyes.

I shut the door behind me. "Your husband is dead."

"Dead," she repeated after me.

"You don't seem surprised."

"Should I be surprised? You don't know the dreams I've been having. It's terrible when you can't quiet your mind, when you're far enough gone to see the faces but you can't quite go to sleep. The faces have been so vivid tonight. I saw his face all bloated by the sea, threatening to devour me."

"Did you hear what I said, Mrs. Sampson? Your husband is dead. He was murdered two hours ago."

"I heard you. I knew I was going to outlive him."

"Is that all it means to you?"

"What more should it mean?" Her voice was blurred and empty of feeling, a wandering sibilance adrift in the deep channel between sleep and waking. "I was widowed before, and I felt it then. When Bob was killed I cried for days. I'm not going to grieve for his father. I wanted him to die."

"You have your wish, then."

"Not all of my wish. He died too soon, or not soon enough. Everybody died too soon. If Miranda had married the other one, Ralph would have changed his will and I'd have it all for myself." She looked up at me slyly. "I know what you must be thinking, Archer. That I'm an evil woman. But I'm not evil really. I have so little, don't you see? I have to look after the little that I have."

"Half of five million dollars," I said.

"It's not the money. It's the power it gives you. I needed it so badly. Now Miranda will go away and leave me all alone. Come and sit beside me for a minute. I have such terrible fears before I go to sleep. Do you think I'll have to see his face every night before I go to sleep?"

"I don't know, Mrs. Sampson." I felt pity for her, but the other feelings were stronger. I went to the door and shut it on her.

Mrs. Kromberg was still in the hall. "I heard you say that Mr. Sampson is dead."

"He is. Mrs. Sampson is too far gone to talk. Do you know where Miranda is?"

"Some place downstairs, I think."

I found her in the living-room, hugging her legs on a hassock beside the fireplace. The lights were out, and through the great central window I could see the dark sea and the silverpoint horizon.

She looked up when I entered the room, but she didn't rise to greet me. "Is that you, Archer?"

"Yes. I have some things to tell you."

"Have you found him?" A glowing log in the fireplace lit up her head and neck with a fitful rosiness. Her eyes were a wide and steady black.

"Yes. He's dead."

"I knew that he'd be dead. He's been dead from the beginning, hasn't he?"

"I wish I could tell you that he had."

"What do you mean?"

I put off explaining what I meant. "I recovered the money."

"The money?"

"This." I tossed the bag at her feet. "The hundred thousand."

"I don't care about it. Where did you find him?"

"Listen to me, Miranda. You're on your own."

"Not entirely," she said. "I married Albert this afternoon."

"I know. He told me. But you've got to get out of this house and look after yourself. The first thing you've got to do is put that money away. I went to a lot of trouble to get it back, and you may be needing part of it."

"I'm sorry. Where shall I put it?"

"The safe in the study, until you can get to a bank."

"All right." She rose with a sudden decisiveness and led the way into the study. Her arms were stiff and her shoulders high, as if they were resisting a downward pressure.

While she was opening the safe I heard a car go down the drive. She turned to me with an awkward movement more appealing than grace. "Who was that?"

"Albert Graves. He drove me out here."

"Why on earth didn't he come in?"

I gathered the remnants of my courage together, and told her: "He killed your father tonight."

Her mouth moved breathlessly and then forced out words. "You're joking, aren't you? He couldn't have."

"He did." I took refuge in facts. "I found out this afternoon where your father was being held. I phoned Graves from Los Angeles and told him to get there as soon as he could, with the sheriff. Graves got there ahead of me, without the sheriff. When I arrived, there was no sign of him. He'd parked his car somewhere out of sight and was still inside the building with your father. When I went inside, he hit me from behind and knocked me out. When I came to, he pretended he'd just arrived. Your father was dead. His body was still warm."

"I can't believe Albert did it."

"You do believe it, though."

"Have you proof?"

"It will have to be technical proof. I had no time to look for it. It's up to the police to find the proof."

She sat down limply in a leather armchair. "So many people have died. Father, and Alan—"

"Graves killed them both."

"But he killed Alan to save you. You told me—"

"It was a complex killing," I said, "a justifiable homicide and something more. He didn't have to kill Taggert. He's a good shot. He could have wounded him. But he wanted Taggert dead. He had his reasons."

"What possible reasons?"

"I think you know of one."

She raised her face in the light. It seemed to me that she had made a choice between a number of different things and settled on boldness. "Yes, I do. I was in love with Alan."

"But you were planning to marry Graves."

"I hadn't made up my mind until last night. I was going to marry someone, and he seemed to be the one. 'It is better to marry than to burn.'"

"He gambled on you, and won. But the other thing he had gambled on didn't happen. Taggert's partner failed to kill your father. So Graves strangled your father himself."

She spread one hand over her eyes and forehead. The blue veins in her temples were young and delicate. "It's incredibly ugly," she said. "I can't understand how he did it."

"He did it for money."

"But he's never cared for money. It's one of the things I

admired in him." She removed her hand from her face, and I saw that she was smiling bitterly. "I haven't been wise in my admirations."

"There may have been a time when Graves didn't care about money. There may be places where he could have stayed that way. Santa Teresa isn't one of them. Money is lifeblood in this town. If you don't have it, you're only half alive. It must have galled him to work for millionaires and handle their money and have nothing of his own. Suddenly he saw his chance to be a millionaire himself. He realized that he wanted money more than anything else on earth."

"Do you know what I wish at this moment?" she said. "I wish I had no money and no sex. They're both more trouble than they're worth to me."

"You can't blame money for what it does to people. The evil is in people, and money is the peg they hang it on. They go wild for money when they've lost their other values."

"I wonder what happened to Albert Graves."

"Nobody knows. He doesn't know himself. The important thing now is what is going to happen to him."

"Do you have to tell the police?"

"I'm going to tell them. It will make it easier for me if you agree. Easier for you in the long run, too."

"You're asking me to share the responsibility, but you don't really care what I think. You're going to tell them anyway. Yet you admit you haven't any proof." She moved restlessly in the chair.

"He won't deny it if he is accused. You know him better than I do."

"I thought I knew him well. Now I'm uncertain—about everything."

"That's why you should let me go ahead. You have doubts to resolve, and you can't resolve them by doing nothing. You can't go on living with uncertainty, either."

"I'm not sure I have to go on living."

"Don't go romantic on me," I said harshly. "Self-pity isn't your way out. You've had terrible luck with two men. I think you're a strong enough girl to take it. I told you before that you've got a life to make. You're on your own."

She inclined toward me. Her breasts leaned out from her body, vulnerable and soft. Her mouth was soft. "I don't know how to begin. What shall I do?"

"Come with me."

"With you? You want me to go with you?"

"Don't try to shift your weight to me, Miranda. You're a lovely girl, and I like you very much, but you're not my baby. Come with me, and we'll talk to the D.A. We'll let him decide."

"Very well. We'll go to Humphreys. He's always been close to Albert."

She drove me up a winding road to the mesa that overlooked the city. When she stopped in front of Humphrey's redwood bungalow, another car was standing in the drive.

"That's Albert's car," she said. "Please go in alone. I don't want to see him."

I left her in the car and climbed the stone steps to the terrace. Humphreys opened the door before I could reach the knocker. His face was more than ever like a skull's.

He stepped out on the terrace and closed the door behind him. "Graves is here," he said. "He came a few minutes ago. He told me he murdered Sampson."

"What are you going to do?"

"I've called the sheriff. He's on his way over." He ran his fingers through his thinning hair. His gestures, like his voice, were light and distant, as if reality had moved back out of his reach. "This is a tragic thing. I believed that Albert Graves was a good man."

"Crime often spreads out like that," I said. "It's epidemic. You've seen it happen before."

"Not to one of my friends." He was silent for a moment. "Bert was talking about Kierkegaard just a minute ago. He quoted something about innocence, that it's like standing on the edge of a deep gulf. You can't look down into the gulf without losing your innocence. Once you've looked, you're guilty. Bert said that he looked down, that he was guilty before he murdered Sampson."

"He's still being easy on himself," I said. "He wasn't looking down; he was looking up. Up to the houses in the hills where the big money lives. He was going to be big himself for a change, with a quarter of Sampson's millions."

Humphreys answered slowly: "I don't know. He never cared for money very much. He still doesn't, I don't think. But something happened to him. He hated Sampson, but so did lots of others. Sampson made anyone who worked for him feel like a valet. But it was something deeper than that in Graves. He'd worked hard all his life, and the whole thing suddenly went sour. It lost its meaning for him. There was no more virtue or justice, in him or in the world. That's why he gave up prosecuting, you know."

"I didn't know."

"Finally he struck out blindly at the world and killed a man."

"Not blindly. Very shrewdly."

"Very blindly," Humphreys said. "I've never seen a man so miserable as Bert Graves is now."

I went back to Miranda. "Graves is here. You weren't entirely wrong about him. He decided to do the right thing."

"Confessed?"

"He was too honest to bluff it through. If nobody had suspected him, he might have. Anyone's honesty has its conditions. But he knew that I knew. He went to Humphreys and told his story."

"I'm glad he did." She denied this a moment later by the sounds she made. Deep shaking sobs bowed her over the wheel.

I lifted her over, and drove myself. As we rolled down the hill, I could see all the lights of the city. They didn't seem quite real. The stars and the house lights were firefly gleams, sparks of cold fire suspended in the black void. The real thing in my world was the girl beside me, warm and shuddering and lost.

I could have put my arms around her and taken her over. She was that lost, that vulnerable. But if I had, she'd have hated me in a week. In six months I might have hated Miranda. I kept my hands to myself and let her lick her wounds. She used my shoulder to cry on as she would have used anyone's.

Her crying was settling down to a steady rhythm, rocking itself to sleep. The sheriff's radio car passed us at the foot of the hill and turned up toward the house where Graves was waiting.

THE LEW ARCHER NOVELS
BY ROSS MACDONALD

"The American private eye, immortalized by Hammett, refined by Chandler, brought to its zenith by Macdonald."
—*The New Tork Times Book Review*

BLACK MONEY

When Lew Archer is hired to get the goods on the suspiciously suave Frenchman who's run off with his client's girlfriend, it looks like a simple case of alienated affections. Things look different when the mysterious foreigner turns out to be connected to a seven-year-old suicide and a mountain of gambling debts.

Crime Fiction/0-679-76810-6

THE CHILL

A distraught young man hires Archer to track down his runaway bride, but no sooner has he found her than Archer finds himself entangled in two murders, one twenty years old, the other so recent that the blood is still warm.

Crime Fiction/0-679-76807-6

THE DROWNING POOL

When a millionaire matriarch is found floating face down in the family pool, the prime suspects are her good-for-nothing son and his seductive teenage daughter. Lew Archer takes this case in the L.A. suburbs and encounters a moral wasteland of corporate greed and family hatred.

Crime Fiction/0-679-76806-8

THE FAR SIDE OF THE DOLLAR

Archer is looking for an unstable rich kid who has run away from an exclusive reform school—and into the arms of kidnappers. Why are his desperate parents so loath to give Archer the information he needs? And why do all trails lead to a derelict Hollywood hotel where starlets and sailors once rubbed elbows with two-bit grifters?

Crime Fiction/0-679-76865-3

THE GALTON CASE

Almost twenty years have passed since Anthony Galton disappeared, along with a suspiciously streetwise bride and several thousand dollars of his family's fortune. Now Anthony's mother wants him back and has hired Lew Archer to find him. What turns up is a headless skeleton, and a boy who claims to be Galton's son.

Crime Fiction/0-679-76864-5

THE MOVING TARGET

She lived in a world of sun, fast cars, and beachfront homes. But when Lew Archer walked in the door, the poor litle rich girl had a problem: her father had been snatched, and a ransom note said cash would get him back.

Crime Fiction/0-375-70146-X

THE UNDERGROUND MAN

As a mysterious fire rages through the hills of a privileged town in Southern California, Archer tracks a missing child who may be the pawn in a marital struggle or the victim of a bizarre kidnapping.

Crime Fiction/0-679-76808-4

THE WYCHERLY WOMAN

Phoebe Wycherly was missing two months before her wealthy father hired Archer to find her. And before he could locate the Wycherly girl, Archer had to reckon with the Wycherly woman, Phoebe's mother, an eerily unmaternal blonde who kept too many residences, had too many secrets, and left too many corpses in her wake.

Crime Fiction/0-375-70144-3

THE ZEBRA-STRIPED HEARSE

It began with a dictatorial father hiring Archer to dig up dirt on his prospective son-in-law, a good-looking painter who might be a genius or a gigolo. But wherever Burke Damis went, Archer kept finding the corpses of people that Damis had taken up and discarded like old clothes.

Crime Fiction/0-375-70145-1